Shadows Revealed

Zora Stone

Print ISBN: 978-1-971405-03-2

Publisher: Smut by Design

www.zorastone.com

Content Warnings

This book contains mature themes, emotional intensity, and explicit content. Please read with care.

Violence & Combat

- On-page death of major antagonists (cosmic/magical destruction)

Mental Health & Trauma

- Intense grief and mourning (on-page, prolonged)

- Emotional breakdowns and psychological processing

- Characters confronting past trauma and violations

- Recovery from survivor's guilt

- Themes of loss, release, and letting go

- Panic responses and emotional overwhelm

Sexual Content

- Explicit sexual scenes between consenting adults

- Multiple romantic/sexual relationships (reverse harem)

- MMF content (male/male/female intimacy)

- MM content (on-page male/male intimacy)

- Group intimacy dynamics

- Detailed intimate encounters with emotional intensity

Magical Coercion & Consent Issues

- Characters explicitly discussing forced magical bonds

- Reckoning with past violations of agency

- Characters confronting those who manipulated their bonds

- Healing and reclaiming autonomy as central theme

Loss & Grief (Heavy)

- Prolonged on-page mourning and emotional processing

- Permanent loss of beloved characters

- Saying goodbye to found family

- Mass souls passing through to the afterlife

- Themes of release, closure, and acceptance

Death & The Afterlife

- Direct interaction with souls and the dead

- Guiding thousands of souls to their final rest

- Witnessing beings pass into the afterlife (peaceful but emotional)

- Cosmic scale of death/souls addressed directly

Cosmic/Existential Themes

- Direct encounter and conversation with a deity

- Questions of fate, purpose, and duty

- Reality-bending magical events

- Ancient mythology revealed and recontextualized

Family Trauma

- Revelation about parents' sacrifice and final moments

- Processing parental loss and legacy

- Discovering the truth about family history

- Healing generational wounds

Deception & Manipulation

- Revelation that major pursuit was an illusion

- Characters processing that they were manipulated

- Confronting the scope of an antagonist's deception

Note: *Shadows Revealed* is an extended epilogue focused on emotional closure, healing, and hope. While it addresses heavy themes of grief and loss, it centers recovery, chosen family, and love after trauma. All romantic relationships occur between consenting adults.

Note 2: This is the final book in the Arcanum Academy series. The story concludes with resolution and healing. The next page contains spoilers from Books One through Three—a quick recap to get you caught up.

A Final Recap from Your Friendly Neighborhood Author

Because *wow*. A lot happened. Patricia filled seventeen notebooks. Bob developed a stress twitch. Even Mouse looked tired, and he's literally immortal.

Let's do this.

So! When we last left our emotionally devastated found family:

Kaia's still the last Valkyrie, still bonded to way too many gorgeous men, and still carrying the Heart of Eternity like the world's most stressful necklace. Her shadows—Bob, Patricia, Finnick, Mouse, and the chaos crew—are still judging everyone. Walter's still doing... whatever Walter does. (Honestly, even I'm not sure. He just vibes and collects things.)

The bonds?

Kieran forced them. All of them. Without consent. Because he's been waiting centuries for Kaia and thought it was the only way to save her life.

She did not take it well.

But here's the thing—throughout Book Three, the bonds started to *heal*. Darian's corruption? Purified. The forced connections? Remade through choice. One by one, they chose each other. For real this time.

The hunt for Seren and Lira:

The group tracked them through Absentia, the corrupted shadow realm where everything is wrong and the vibes are immaculate (if you like existential dread). Weeks of desperate searching. Weeks of Kaia refusing to give up on her friends.

It led them straight to the Gate.

Oh, and Malrik and Darian are half-brothers.

Same father. The Shadow King of Absentia. Alekir dropped *that* little bomb mid-confrontation at the Gate because he's exactly that kind of villain. Something about choosing Darian specifically because he was "Malrik's." Because the corruption was never random—it was personal.

They're... processing.

Callum?

Betrayed them all. Kieran trusted him completely. That trust was misplaced. File that under "things that left scars."

The Gate:

They found it. The ancient doorway between life and death, sealed for centuries. And with six bloodlines aligned—Light, Shadow, Chaos, Elemental, Berserker, Shifter—all connected to Kaia, all bound by choice...

It opened.

Alekir, the Soulbinder?

Showed up expecting victory. Centuries of planning. Generations of manipulation. The corruption, the forced bonds, the hunt—all designed to bring Kaia here, to use her to free the God of Chaos and destroy everything.

He got exactly what he wanted.

Sort of.

The God of Chaos emerged.

And He was *not* what Alekir expected.

The God does not tolerate nonsense.

And then Kaia turned around.

Behind her stood a wall of shadows. Bob and Patricia and Mouse at the front. Walter pulsing bright. The named shadows holding formation like they'd been waiting for this moment.

And behind *them*?

Thousands. Hundreds of thousands. So many shadows they blocked out the sky. Souls who've been waiting since the Gate closed. Since the Valkyries fell. Since the bridge between life and death collapsed and left them with nowhere to go.

They weren't there to fight.

They were there to go *home*.

And they were all bowing.

Book Three ended with Kaia and an army of souls at her back, a God who's been waiting centuries, and a purpose she never asked for but was always meant to fulfill.

Ready for Book Four?

Because the goodbyes are just beginning.

And some of them are going to *hurt*.

CONTENTS

Chapter 1
KAIA

I'm ready to die.

For Finn, who loved me before I loved myself. Who made me laugh when the world was falling apart. Who's still holding my wrist like he can anchor me to this life through sheer stubbornness.

For Torric, who burns so hot and loves so fierce. Who would set the world on fire if it meant keeping me safe.

For Aspen, who steadies me with a touch. Who sees me — really sees me — and stays anyway.

For Malrik, who leads when no one asks him to. Who carries weight he never signed up for. Who calls me Nightshade like it's a prayer.

For Darian, who clawed his way back from corruption. Who chose us. Who chose *me*.

For Kieran, who's waited centuries. Who's made mistakes he can't take back. Who loves me in a language older than words.

For Bob and Mouse and Walter and Patricia. For Finnick and Carl and Steve and Linda. For all the Eds who followed without question.

None of them deserve to die for something that started centuries before I was born.

None of them need to die for me.

But they will.

I see it in the way they're positioned — six men ready to form a wall between me and a god. I feel it through the bonds — six hearts ready to stop beating if it means mine keeps going.

That's the thought crystallizing in my chest as I face the God of Chaos, wings spread, power still crackling through my veins.

We won't survive this.

But we'll go down together.

The God watches me with those ancient, endless eyes. Reality bends around him like heat shimmer off summer stone. The plateau holds its breath.

And then—

"Turn around."

His voice is quiet. Not the thunder I expected. Not rage or condemnation or divine judgment.

Just... instruction.

I don't move. Can't. Every muscle locked, every instinct screaming that if I take my eyes off him for one second—

"Kaia."

My name in his mouth feels like being seen by the universe itself.

"Turn around."

Finn's fingers tighten on my wrist. I feel his chaos magic trembling against my skin — not a warning. An encouragement.

Trust this.

I turn.

And I stop breathing.

They're still there.

The shadows. The army. The thousands upon thousands of souls that materialized while I was facing the God.

But now — with my wings still humming, with the alignment still singing through my blood — I see them differently.

At the front: my shadows. My *named* shadows.

Walter hovers, pulsing violet — brighter than I've ever seen him, his strange light flaring in recognition. Mouse sits sentinel beside him, panther-sized and ancient. Bob's massive form anchors the line, sharp-edged and proud, flanked by Patricia with her glowing notebook and Finnick who's somehow doing a slow clap even now. Linda and Steve and Carl hold formation behind them.

They have presence. Weight. *Personality.*

They're not just shadows.

They're Valkyries. True Valkyrie souls who chose to bind themselves to my line centuries ago. My sisters.

And behind them—

Eds.

Thousands of them. Hundreds of thousands. So many they block out the dying light. So many they've swallowed the plateau and the mountain and everything beyond.

Just... Eds.

Faceless. Identical. An endless sea of shadow forms that blur together into a cosmic backlog. Souls who couldn't pass through when the Gate closed. They've simply... waited. Instinct holding them here. Patient in the way only the dead can be patient — without awareness, without suffering, just *existing* until the door opened again.

The contrast almost makes me laugh. My named shadows — distinct, fierce, *real* — standing guard over an army of... Eds.

They stretch back across the plateau, down the mountain, into the valleys below. So many the snow has disappeared beneath them. So many I can't see where they end.

And every single one of them is bowed.

The named shadows at the front — Bob's crisp salute, Patricia's respectful incline, Mouse's ancient nod.

And behind them, a wave of Eds all doing the same thing. Bowing. In that vaguely synchronized way that suggests they're not entirely sure what's happening but everyone else is doing it so they probably should too.

The kind of bow you give to royalty. To saviors.

To someone you've been waiting for.

"Holy shit," Finn breathes.

Then, quieter, tugging on my wrist like an excited toddler at a parade: "Kaia... there are SO. MANY. EDS."

Torric swears in a language I don't recognize.

Aspen says nothing, but I feel his awe crash through the bond like a wave.

Malrik steps closer. Not speaking. Just there. A solid presence at my shoulder.

"They're bowing to him," I whisper. "The God. They're—"

"No."

The voice comes from behind me. Close now. Closer than before.

I spin back, heart slamming against my ribs.

The God of Chaos stands ten feet away, the tension from before gone.

His weathered face holds something I didn't expect. Something that looks almost like sorrow. Or maybe wonder. It's hard to read expressions on a being older than time.

"Little Valkyrie." He tilts his head, studying me like I'm a puzzle he's finally solved. "They are not bowing for me."

The words don't make sense.

"Then who—"

"You."

Nope.

My wings flicker. My knees threaten to buckle.

"That's not— I didn't—"

"You did."

He begins to move. Circling me the way a teacher circles a student, each step measured, patient.

"You did what no one else could do. What no one else *can* do." He gestures toward the open Gate, still blazing white against the black stone. "Only a Valkyrie could reopen this. Only one bound to both life and death."

Another step closer.

"You faced Alekir." His voice carries soft disdain — the dismissal of a god for an old little man who thought himself important. "You faced your fears. And you followed your heart — even when it led you here. Even when it asked you to risk everything."

He stops in front of me. Close enough to touch.

"You didn't know what waited on the other side of that choice." Something shifts in his ancient face. Almost gentle. "You chose anyway. That is what makes you worthy."

My throat closes. Tears burn behind my eyes.

"I didn't know," I manage. "I didn't plan any of this—"

"No." His gaze holds mine. "You didn't know. You loved. You trusted. And you opened the door."

Behind me, I feel my men processing. Their emotions crash through the connection — shock, awe, pride, love, fear, hope.

Finn's voice, barely audible: "Kaia... they were waiting for *you*?"

Torric's jaw clenches, but pride radiates through the bond like heat.

Aspen breathes my name like a prayer.

Darian's light flickers. Not fear this time. Wonder.

And Kieran—

Kieran's dragon form lowers. Massive head dipping toward the snow. Wings folding against his scaled body.

He's bowing.

To me.

A dragon. An ancient being who's lived centuries. Who's watched empires rise and fall.

He's given me his devotion. His protection. His heart.

But this — this physical surrender, scales and wings and ancient power pressing toward the snow — this is something else. Something I've never seen from him.

The bond between us floods with it. Not new devotion — that's always been there.

Acknowledgment.

Of what I am. Of what I've become.

Complete and absolute.

My chest cracks open.

Around us, the others react — Torric's sharp intake of breath, Aspen's stillness going somehow *stiller*, Malrik's shadows rippling with something that looks like shock. Even Darian's light wavers.

A dragon doesn't bow.

Kieran just did.

"I don't understand," I whisper. "I'm just—"

"You are the last." The God's voice cuts through my spiral. "The last true Valkyrie. The last who can guide them home."

He looks past me, toward the army of shadows still pressed to the snow.

"Your line created the Gate. Built the bridge between life and death. And when Alekir destroyed your people, when he trapped their souls and broke the cycle..." His ancient eyes return to mine. "The Gate closed. The bridge collapsed. And they had nowhere to go."

I turn back to face them.

My named shadows at the front — sisters who chose me.

And behind them, thousands upon thousands of Eds. Souls who just need to get through. Who've been stuck in cosmic limbo because the door was locked and nobody had the key.

Until now.

The tears spill over. I can't stop them. Don't try.

"This whole time," I breathe. "They've been here this whole time."

"Yes."

The God moves to stand beside me.

"Your shadows knew." He gestures toward where Walter hovers, pulsing brighter now — his violet light flaring twice like a heartbeat. Where Mouse presses against my leg, solid and warm. Where Bob holds the line, his sharp edges softening as I meet his form.

"They weren't strategizing," the God continues. "They were following the pull. The call of the Valkyrie soul they're bound to. They gathered the lost because *you* called to them — even when you didn't know you were calling."

Walter. Sweet, strange, cosmic Walter. Drifting through our journey, pulsing at objects, collecting fragments I didn't understand.

He wasn't just existing.

He was answering me.

Building this.

Because I needed it.

"Kaia." The God's voice softens. "Do not shrink from what you are."

I swallow hard. Force myself to breathe.

"What happens now?"

He lifts one weathered hand. Not commanding. Welcoming.

And his expression shifts — ancient and knowing, like someone who has been waiting a very long time to see this moment.

"Now?" He gestures toward the Gate. Toward the blazing white light. Toward whatever waits on the other side. "Now you do what Valkyries have always done."

He turns to face the shadow army. The souls. The lost.

His voice carries across the plateau — not loud, but infinite. Reaching every bowed figure, every waiting spirit, every Ed who's held on for centuries.

"Rise."

They do.

Slowly. Reverently. The named shadows first — Bob snapping to attention, Patricia tucking her notebook away, Mouse stretching like he's been waiting for this his whole existence. Walter pulses once, twice, bright and steady.

And then the Eds. Rising in a wave. Tens of thousands of identical shadow forms straightening up, shuffling slightly, ready to finally *move*.

Thousands of faces turn toward me. The named shadows with expressions I can read — pride, hope, love. The Eds with... well. Ed expressions. Vaguely patient. Vaguely ready to get this whole "being dead" thing sorted out.

The God looks at me one last time.

"Come, Valkyrie. Your dead are waiting."

The Gate pulses behind us. Its hum deepens — a sound I feel in my bones more than hear. The light shifts from blinding white to something warmer. Something that feels like welcome.

Like home.

Chapter 2
FINN

There are so many Eds.

I cannot stress this enough.

SO. MANY. EDS.

They're shuffling toward the Gate like the world's longest, most depressing conga line. Thousands of identical shadow blobs, indistinguishable from each other, moving with all the urgency of a glacier with commitment issues.

Kaia stands at the threshold, wings spread, looking like a goddess made of starlight and shadow.

And the Eds just... shuffle past her.

One of them bumps into another. They both wobble. Neither acknowledges it.

"This is the most anticlimactic apocalypse I've ever seen," I say.

Torric grunts. "Shut up, Finn."

"No, seriously. We fought a god. Okay, we didn't, but we would have. We aligned six bloodlines. We literally opened a Gate to the afterlife. And now we're watching—" I gesture at the endless stream of identical shadows. "—traffic."

An Ed shuffles past. Then another. Then three more in a clump that looks suspiciously like they're trying to cut in line.

"Bye, Ed," I call out.

The Ed doesn't respond. Obviously. It's an Ed.

"Farewell, Ed. Enjoy being dead somewhere else."

Another Ed passes. This one seems to be moving slower than the others. Taking its time. Sightseeing on its way to the afterlife.

"Pick up the pace, Ed. You're holding up the line."

Bob materializes beside me. His posture radiates disapproval.

"What? Someone should say goodbye. It's polite."

Bob's form ripples in a way that clearly says *I did not bind my immortal soul to the Valkyrie line for this.*

"See you later, Ed. Have a good one, Ed. Tell the other side Finn says hi."

Patricia appears on my other side, notebook out, scribbling furiously.

"Are you documenting this?"

She doesn't look up. Just keeps writing.

"Patricia. Are you writing down my Ed farewells?"

More scribbling.

"That's going in the historical record, isn't it? 'Finn Veylan, legendary chaos mage, talked shit to eight thousand dead people.'"

Scribble scribble scribble.

"I'm going to be a footnote. A really embarrassing footnote."

An Ed bumps into the Ed in front of it. The first Ed wobbles. The second Ed wobbles. A third Ed, seemingly unrelated to the collision, also wobbles.

"Did you see that?" I point. "That Ed just caused a three-Ed pileup. That's a multi-Ed collision. An Ed-cident."

Torric pinches the bridge of his nose. "I'm going to kill you."

"You can't. I'm essential to the polycule. Also, Kaia would be sad."

"She'd get over it."

"Rude."

Another Ed shuffles past. This one has a weird lump on its head. Or maybe that's just how Eds look. Hard to tell. They're very... Ed-shaped.

"Hey, Lumpy Ed. Looking good. Love what you've done with your... lump."

Aspen appears at my shoulder, quiet as always. "Are you naming them?"

"What? No. They're all Ed. That's the point. They're Eds."

"You called that one Lumpy Ed."

"That's a descriptor, not a name. Totally different."

Another Ed passes. This one seems to be moving sideways somehow. Diagonally. Against the flow of Ed-traffic.

"Where's that one going? Ed. Ed, buddy. The Gate's that way. You're going the wrong—and he's gone. Okay. Godspeed, Diagonal Ed. You do you."

Movement to my left.

The God is walking toward us.

Not toward Kaia. Toward *us*.

My chaos magic coils tight, uncertain. Every instinct screaming that when an actual deity approaches, you should probably stop making fun of dead people.

But he's not looking at me.

He's looking at Kaia.

Watching her stand at the threshold, wings pulsing with light, guiding souls home like she was born for it. Which, I guess, she was.

His expression is... soft. Almost fond.

Then his gaze slides to me, and something shifts in those ancient eyes. Amusement, maybe. Recognition.

"Eds," he says.

I blink. "What?"

"You call them Eds." He gestures at the endless stream of shadows. "Why?"

"I... uh..." Suddenly my mouth is very dry. "Because there's a lot of them? And they all look the same? And naming them individually seemed like a commitment I wasn't ready to make?"

The God of Chaos laughs.

Actually *laughs*.

It sounds like thunder rolling through a canyon. Like stars colliding. Like the universe itself finding something genuinely funny.

"Eds," he repeats, still chuckling. "Millions of souls, waiting centuries to pass through... and you call them Eds."

"Should I... not?"

"No, no." He waves a weathered hand. "It's perfect. Very chaos."

His eyes drift back to Kaia. Watching. Always watching.

The others have noticed. Torric moves closer, fire banked but ready. Aspen drifts to my other side. Malrik's shadows coil around his feet as he approaches. Darian's light flickers, uncertain. Even Kieran steps in, forming a loose circle around the God and me.

Everyone except Kaia.

She's still at the Gate. Still guiding. Still glowing.

She can't hear this.

"You know," the God says, his voice casual in that way that makes my spine lock up, "I've watched many chaos wielders over the centuries. Millions of them. All of them touched by my essence, whether they knew it or not."

He's looking at me now. Really looking. Those ancient eyes pinning me in place.

"But you, Finn Veylan..." He tilts his head. "You're different."

"Different good or different 'about to be smited'?"

"Smote."

"What?"

"The past tense is smote. And no." His gaze drifts back to Kaia. Lingers there. "Different *important*."

Torric shifts. I feel his heat flare, protective. "What do you mean?"

The God doesn't answer immediately. Just watches Kaia guide another wave of Eds through the Gate. Her wings pulse. The light shifts.

"Do you know why your magic always felt wrong, Finn?"

I don't know what to say to that.

Because yes. Fuck yes, I know. I've always known something was off. Always felt like my chaos was working overtime, straining against something I couldn't see or understand. Everyone told me I was unstable. Dangerous. Broken.

"It was doing its job," the God says quietly. "The whole time."

"What job?"

He turns to face me fully. The others press closer. Listening.

"When Solveig used the Heart of Eternity to send her daughter through time, the magic was... imprecise. Chaotic." A faint smile. "Time magic always is. Kaia could have landed anywhere. Any realm. Any century. Scattered across infinity like smoke in wind."

My chest is tight. My magic is writhing.

"But she didn't," I manage.

"No. She didn't." His ancient eyes hold mine. "Because something caught her. Gave her a direction. A destination. An anchor point to pull her through safely."

"What..." I can barely get the word out. "What caught her?"

The God smiles. Gentle. Almost paternal.

"You did."

The world stops.

"You were young. Eight, perhaps. Maybe ten. Your chaos magic had just awakened, wild and uncontrolled and *reaching*." He glances at Kaia again. "It reached across time. Across realms. Found a six-year-old girl hurtling through the void with nowhere to land."

"I don't... I don't understand."

"Your magic gave her a way out, Finn. Before you knew what chaos was. Before you knew her name. Your power reached into the space between worlds and said *here — come here — I've got you*."

I can't breathe.

"And she did," the God continues. "She landed safely. In the right place. The right time. A realm where she could grow up, where she could become who she needed to be. Because your magic pulled her through."

Torric's hand lands on my shoulder. Warm. Grounding.

I barely feel it.

"But chaos magic doesn't let go easily," the God says. "Once it finds something, it holds on. Your power stayed connected to her across years. Always reaching. Always searching for the girl it had saved."

"The strain," I whisper. "The wrongness—"

"Was your magic stretched thin. Tethered to a Valkyrie you'd never met, waiting for the day she'd finally appear."

The tears come before I can stop them.

All those years.

All those years of being told I was broken. Unstable. Dangerous. A liability.

And I was reaching for her.

I was *finding* her.

"The day she appeared at your academy," the God says, "your magic didn't react because she was powerful or interesting or new. It reacted because it could finally *stop reaching*. She was here. She was real. She was found."

His ancient eyes meet mine.

"Your magic didn't scream 'finally' because of attraction, Finn. It screamed 'finally' because after years of holding on... it could rest. She was *home.*"

Aspen's frost brushes my arm. Cool. Calming.

Malrik's shadows brush against my skin. Steadying.

Darian's light flickers, warm and golden.

Kieran says nothing, but I feel his presence, his understanding.

"That's why your magic screamed when she appeared," the God says. "Not *finally* as in 'finally something interesting.' *Finally* as in... reunion. As in 'I've been holding you for years and now I can see your face.'"

I'm shaking.

Full-body shaking.

"She doesn't know?" My voice cracks. "Kaia doesn't—"

"No." The God looks at her again. Still guiding. Still glowing. Oblivious to everything happening behind her. "That's not my truth to tell. It's yours."

He steps back. Gives me space.

"You asked what you are, Finn Veylan. You're the boy who saved a Valkyrie before he knew Valkyries existed. You're the chaos that held when everything else fell apart."

He turns to walk away. Pauses.

"You're not my descendant by blood," he adds, almost as an afterthought. "But you carry my essence better than anyone I've seen in millennia. That magic of yours — the chaos everyone feared — it's not a flaw."

His ancient eyes meet mine one last time.

"It's a gift."

Then he's gone. Walking back toward the Gate. Toward Kaia.

I stand there.

Shaking.

The others close in around me. A wall of warmth and shadow and light and frost. Protecting me from nothing. From everything.

"Finn." Torric's voice is rough. "You okay?"

I laugh. It comes out wet and broken.

"I saved her." The words feel impossible. Holy. "I *saved* her. Before I knew her. Before I loved her. I was already—"

I can't finish.

Aspen's hand finds mine. Cold fingers threading through my shaking ones.

"You were already hers," he says quietly. "And she was already yours."

I look at Kaia.

My Trouble. My Valkyrie. The girl I've been holding together since I was a child.

She's still at the Gate. Still guiding. Wings pulsing, face calm, tears drying on her cheeks.

She has no idea.

No idea what I did. What I've been doing. What my magic has been screaming about since the moment she walked into my life.

I wipe my face. Take a breath.

"Bye, Ed."

The word comes out steadier than I expected.

Another Ed shuffles past. Then another.

"See you later, Ed."

Torric's hand squeezes my shoulder.

"Safe travels, Ed."

Malrik's shadows brush my ankles. Gentle.

"Thanks for waiting, Ed."

Aspen doesn't let go of my hand.

"She came for you."

Darian's light pulses warm.

"She finally came."

I keep saying goodbye.

But it feels different now.

I'm not joking anymore.

I'm not crying anymore either.

I'm just... here. Standing with my brothers. Watching the woman I saved before I knew her name guide the dead to their rest.

"Hey, Ed?"

The next shadow pauses. Almost like it's listening. Probably not. It's an Ed.

"When you get to the other side? Tell them about her." My voice is steady now. Strong. "Tell them a Valkyrie came back. Tell them she had help."

The Ed shuffles past. Disappears into the light.

Another takes its place.

Then another.

Then a thousand more.

"Bye, Ed," I whisper. "Bye."

The Gate pulses.

The Eds keep coming.

And I keep saying goodbye.

But now I know why I'm here.

Now I know what I've always been.

Not broken.

Not unstable.

Not wrong.

Hers.

Chapter 3
MALRIK

I can't stop watching him.

Finn stands at the edge of our group, shoulders curved inward like he's trying to make himself smaller. The others have given him space — Torric a few feet to his left, Aspen just behind, Darian hovering with that uncertain light of his.

But I'm the one who can't look away.

My shadow magic flickers at my edges, restless. Responding to something I haven't let myself name yet.

The God's words echo through my skull.

Your magic found her. Before you knew her name. Your power reached into the space between worlds and said here — come here — I've got you.

Finn. Chaotic, ridiculous, insufferable Finn.

The man who deflects pain with humor and hides heartbreak behind a smile.

He's been holding Kaia together since he was a child. Carrying a weight none of us knew existed. Reaching across time and space for a girl he'd never met, tethering her to safety while everyone around him called him broken.

And he never said a word.

Never asked for help.

Never stopped *reaching*.

Something clicks into place in my chest.

I breathe deep as recognition hits me.

I'm in love with him.

I don't know when it started. Maybe the first time he made Kaia laugh when she was falling apart. Maybe the first time his chaos magic sparked against my shadows and I felt something *answer*. Maybe it's been building since the beginning and I was too focused on strategy, on survival, on Kaia to see it.

But I see it now.

I love Kaia with everything I am. That hasn't changed. Won't ever change.

And I love him too.

Different. Equal. *His*.

The Eds continue their endless shuffle toward the Gate. Thousands of identical shadows, faceless and patient, streaming past Kaia like a river around a stone. She stands at the threshold, wings spread, guiding them home.

She doesn't know.

She doesn't know what Finn did. What he's been doing. What his magic has been screaming about since the moment she walked into his life.

But I know.

And I can't unknow it.

His hands won't stop trembling. His chaos magic sparks and fizzles, exhausted. His eyes are red-rimmed, wet, and he keeps blinking like he's trying to hold himself together through sheer force of will.

Torric catches my eye. He shifts his weight, creating an opening.

Aspen does the same. A subtle repositioning that says *go*.

I don't hesitate.

I walk toward him. Finn looks up as I approach, and his expression — devastated, vulnerable, *wrecked* — nearly stops me in my tracks.

"Hey, Malrik." His voice cracks. Tries to be light. Fails. "Come to watch the Ed parade? It's very exciting. That one just bumped into that other one. Riveting stuff."

I don't take the deflection.

I step into his space. Close. Closer than I've ever let myself get.

"Finn."

His jaw tightens. The tremor in his hands gets worse.

"I'm fine," he says. "Totally fine. Just learned I've been magically tethered to the love of my life since childhood, no big deal. Happens to everyone. Very normal Tuesday."

"It's not Tuesday."

"Whatever day it is, then. Point stands."

He's trying so hard. Working so hard to be okay. To be the one who makes everyone else feel better.

I reach out. Cup his face in my hands.

He freezes.

"You've carried her longer than any of us," I say quietly. "Longer than anyone should have as a child, especially alone."

His breath catches. His green eyes go wide.

"Let someone carry you for a while."

"Malrik—" His voice breaks. "I'm not— I don't need— it's fine. I'm *fine.*"

"You're not fine." I brush my thumb across his cheekbone. Feel the dampness there. "And you don't have to be."

Something cracks in his expression.

"She doesn't know yet." My voice drops. Just for him. "But I do. And I won't forget."

"I didn't know." The words come out ragged. "My whole life, my magic felt wrong. Like it was stretched too thin. Like it was looking for something I couldn't find. And now I find out—" His voice cracks. "I was holding onto *her.* Since I was a kid. And I didn't even know she existed."

I kiss him.

I kiss him like I should have kissed him weeks ago. Like I should have kissed him in the hot spring. Like I've wanted to every time he made me laugh, every time he looked at me with those sharp green eyes, every time his chaos sparked against my shadows and made something in my chest ache.

Finn makes a sound against my mouth — broken and surprised and *hungry* — and then he's kissing me back.

His hands fist in my shirt. His chaos magic flares wild, crackling against my skin. I feel it everywhere — in my chest, in my shadows, in the bond that hums between us.

He tastes like salt and desperation and something underneath that's purely *Finn*.

When we break apart, we're both breathing hard.

His forehead drops against mine. His eyes are closed. His hands are still shaking, but he's holding onto me like I'm the only solid thing in the world.

"Malrik." My name comes out wrecked. "*Malrik*."

"I've got you." I wrap my arms around him. Pull him close. Let him bury his face in my neck. "I've got you."

He breaks.

Not loudly. Not dramatically.

Just a shudder that runs through his whole body. A sob he tries to swallow. A collapse into my arms that says he's been holding himself together for so long and he just... can't anymore.

I hold him tighter.

"You held her," I murmur against his hair. "Now let me hold you."

His arms wrap around me. Desperate. Clinging.

"I didn't know," he whispers. "I didn't know what I was doing. I just felt her and I didn't even know it was her. I couldn't let go and everyone said I was broken but I *couldn't let go—*"

"You weren't broken." I press a kiss to his temple. "You were saving her."

"I was just a kid."

"You were extraordinary." I pull back just enough to look at him. Cup his face again. Make him meet my eyes. "You *are* extraordinary. And you have no idea, do you? No idea what you did. What you've always been."

His eyes are wet. His lip trembles.

"Malrik..."

"I love you."

The words come out before I can stop them. Before I can strategize or calculate or control.

Finn stops breathing.

"I love Kaia," I continue, steady now. Certain. "And I love you. Not the same. Not less. Just... yours."

He stares at me. Those green eyes wide and wet and *shattered*.

"You can't just— you can't just *say* that—"

"I can. I did." I brush my thumb across his cheek again. "And I'll say it again, as many times as you need to hear it."

He laughs. Broken and wet and disbelieving.

Then he kisses me.

Softer this time. Slower. His hands come up to frame my face the way I'm framing his, and we just... breathe each other in.

Behind us, I'm vaguely aware of the others shifting. Giving us space. Guarding without crowding.

When we finally pull apart, Finn's breathing has steadied. His chaos magic has calmed to a low hum. He's still shaking, but it's different now.

Not alone.

"Bye, Ed."

The whisper comes from him. Soft. Almost automatic.

I glance at the Gate. Another Ed shuffles past Kaia into the light.

"Later, Ed," Finn murmurs. His head is still against my shoulder. His fingers are still tangled in my shirt.

I press a kiss to his hair.

"Take your time."

He laughs. Watery but real.

"There are like a million more Eds, Malrik. We're going to be here forever."

"Then we'll be here forever."

He goes quiet. His hand tightens in my shirt.

"You meant it?" His voice is small. Vulnerable. "What you said?"

"Every word."

"Even the love part?"

"Especially the love part."

He exhales. Long and shaky.

"I love you too," he whispers. "I think I have for a while. I just... didn't think..."

"Didn't think what?"

"That anyone would want me like that. The real me. Not the jokes. Not the deflection. Just... me."

My chest cracks open.

"Finn." I tilt his chin up. Make him look at me. "I want every part of you. The jokes. The chaos. The boy who saved a Valkyrie before he knew what a Valkyrie was. All of it."

His eyes fill again.

"You're going to make me cry again."

"I'll hold you through that too."

He laughs. Wet and broken and *happy*.

Then he tucks his head back against my shoulder and watches the Eds shuffle past.

"Bye, Ed," he whispers.

I hold him tighter.

"Bye, Ed," I echo.

And we stand there together — watching the dead march into the afterlife, surrounded by our family, with Kaia glowing at the threshold and a million Eds still waiting their turn.

I don't know what comes next.

I don't know what any of this means for us. For the bonds. For the future.

But right now, with Finn in my arms and my heart cracked open in the best way, I don't want anything else.

Chapter 4
KAIA

My wings hurt.

I didn't even know wings could hurt, but here we are. Standing at the edge of eternity with aching wing-muscles and tear tracks drying on my face and an endless parade of Eds still shuffling past me into the light.

This is my life now, apparently. Professional Ed-watcher. Cosmic crossing guard.

Behind me, the bonds hum steady and warm. Finn's chaos feels different somehow — brighter, more settled — I'm going to have to ask him about that. Malrik feels almost content. Torric and Aspen struggle with the need to protect me even now. And Kieran? He's ready to go home, but refuses to leave me.

They're all still here.

We're still here.

Thank the gods.

Another Ed shuffles past. I've stopped counting. Stopped saying good-bye to each one. My voice gave out about an hour ago.

Movement to my left, and the God steps up beside me. He doesn't crowd. Doesn't speak. Just exists there, watching the souls pass with an expression I can't read.

I should probably be terrified of him. I was, like, two hours ago. Now I'm just tired.

"You did well, Little Valkyrie."

The words hit somewhere I wasn't expecting. Somewhere soft and bruised that I thought I'd armored over.

My throat goes tight.

"I didn't do anything," I manage. "I just stood here."

"You opened the Gate. Aligned six bloodlines through choice. Faced a monster who spent centuries preparing for this moment." He glances at me, and there's something almost warm in those ancient eyes. "You did not break."

"I almost broke."

"Almost is not the same as did."

I don't have a comeback for that.

More Eds shuffle past. The stream is thinning — I can see gaps between them now. Spaces where snow peeks through.

My chest tightens.

"Can I ask you something?"

He inclines his head.

"Seren and Lira." The names scrape out of me. "We followed them through Absentia. We saw them. Heard them. They were *here*." I wave at the Gate, at the stragglers still passing through. "But they haven't come through. Where are they? Did I miss them? Did something happen? Are they—"

"You never followed them."

My stomach drops straight through my feet.

"What?"

"The Seren and Lira you saw were fabrications." His voice is gentle, which somehow makes it worse. "Illusions woven from your memories. Bait."

No.

No, that's not—

We *saw* them. We tracked them for weeks. I pushed everyone to the breaking point trying to reach them—

"Alekir knew you would follow them," the God continues. "Knew it would break you open. Drive you closer to the Gate." A pause. "He showed you what you feared most. What you wanted most."

I can't breathe.

"None of it was real."

The words land like a punch to the chest.

"They were never in Absentia," he says quietly. "Their souls were never trapped here. Alekir did not have them."

"Then where—"

"Safe. At the academy."

I don't know if I want to scream or collapse or laugh until I can't stop.

All those weeks. All that guilt. All those nights lying awake convinced I was failing them, that they were suffering somewhere I couldn't reach, that it was my fault—

"I thought I failed them." My voice cracks and I hate it. "I thought—"

"You couldn't have saved them here. There was nothing to save them from."

The relief hits so hard my knees almost buckle.

They're safe.

Seren and Lira are *safe*.

I didn't fail them because they were never here to fail.

A sob rips out of me before I can stop it. Then another. I press my hands over my face and just let it happen because I'm too tired to pretend anymore.

The God doesn't touch me. Doesn't offer platitudes.

He just waits.

When I finally get myself together — mostly — I wipe my face and look back at the Gate. The Eds are still coming, but barely. A trickle now instead of a flood.

"How many more?" My voice sounds wrecked.

The God glances at the remaining souls, then at me. Something shifts in his expression.

"Would you like me to speed this along?"

"What?"

He raises one hand.

Snaps his fingers.

And every remaining Ed on the plateau — thousands of them — just... ripples. Like wind through grass. Like a wave pulling back from shore.

Then they're gone.

All of them. Swept through the Gate in one gentle rush.

The plateau goes silent. Empty. Snow and stone and nothing else.

I stare at the space where an army of souls stood two seconds ago.

"Hey!" Finn's voice cuts across the plateau, indignant and bewildered. "The Eds! Where did they— I wasn't done! I had a whole speech prepared for Ed number five hundred thousand!"

Gods, I love him.

I turn back to the God, pretty sure my expression is somewhere between incredulous and murderous.

"You could have done that the whole time?"

"Yes."

"Then why didn't you—"

"You seemed very determined." The faintest hint of a smile. "Your ancestors always preferred ceremony."

"I had *material*," Finn calls out, still sounding betrayed. "Good material. Ed-specific material."

I shake my head at Finn's antics. But honestly, I don't know whether to laugh or punch an ancient deity.

"I've been standing here for hours."

"I noticed."

"Saying goodbye to individual Eds. My voice gave out. My wings hurt."

"Also noticed."

"And you just—" I gesture wildly at the empty plateau. "One finger snap. That's all it took."

"Would you have wanted me to do it earlier?"

I open my mouth. Close it.

Because no. I wouldn't have. Those hours meant something, even if I can't explain what.

"No," I admit, hating that he's right. "I wouldn't have."

He nods like that settles it.

I turn to look out over Absentia, mostly to avoid his smug ancient face.

And my breath catches.

It's changing.

Right now, in real time, the gray wasteland I've been traveling through for weeks is waking up. Patches of green breaking through dead stone. Hills shifting from ash to moss and gold. Rivers shaking off their darkness and running clear.

Trees bursting into color — reds and golds and deep greens — like someone flipped a switch marked "autumn" and the whole realm responded.

"It's beautiful," I whisper.

"It always wanted to be." The God steps up beside me. "The corruption kept it frozen. Now that the Gate is open, now that souls can pass through again…" He gestures at the healing landscape. "Balance returns."

I watch a hillside bloom gold. Watch a river run silver. Watch the world become what it was supposed to be.

My parents never got to see this.

The thought rises unbidden, and suddenly my chest is too tight again.

"My parents," I say quietly. "Did they know? When they sent me through? Did they know any of this would happen?"

The God is quiet for a long moment.

"They knew you would live."

Something cracks behind my ribs.

"They sent you through time because it was the only door Alekir couldn't follow you through. The only way to save you." His voice is soft in a way that makes my eyes burn. "They never regretted the choice. Not for one moment."

I can't look at him. Can't look at anything. My vision is blurring.

"They didn't die in despair, Kaia. They died in hope."

A sound escapes me. Something between a sob and a laugh.

"You were their last thought." The God's voice drops even quieter. "And their first prayer."

I break.

Not dramatically. Not loudly. Just tears streaming down my face and my shoulders shaking and centuries of grief finally having somewhere to go.

They died hoping I would live.

They died believing I would become this.

"Thank you," I manage when I can speak again. The words feel tiny against everything he's given me. "For telling me that."

He inclines his head.

Then he steps back a few feet. Gives me space.

But he doesn't leave.

I can feel him there, waiting. Because he's not done. There's more coming — I can feel it in the way he's watching me, in the way the bonds are humming, in the way Absentia keeps unfurling beneath us like it's been holding its breath for centuries.

But for now, I just stand here.

Watching the world heal.

Feeling Finn's chaos spark bright and strange in my chest — different than before, happier somehow — and making a mental note to find out what the hell happened while I was busy being a professional Ed-watcher.

The wind carries the smell of growing things. Of life coming back.

Behind me, my men wait.

Ahead of me, Absentia blooms.

And for the first time in longer than I can remember, I feel like maybe — *maybe* — everything is going to be okay.

Chapter 5
KAIA

The plateau is quiet in a way that makes my ears ring.

No more shuffling. No more Eds. Just wind and snow and the Gate humming behind me like a heartbeat that isn't mine.

And my shadows.

They're all standing in a line.

Not scattered around the plateau like usual. Not doing their own thing — Bob organizing, Patricia scribbling, Finnick causing problems, Carl falling out of something.

They're just... standing there.

Watching me.

Mouse at the front, panther-sized and ancient. Walter hovering beside him, pulsing brighter than I've ever seen. Bob at rigid attention, edges sharp enough to cut. Patricia with her notebook closed — *closed* — pressed against her chest. Finnick actually still for once. Carl managing not to trip over anything. Steve standing straight, Linda beside him with her hand on his shoulder like she's keeping him steady.

They're all looking between me and the Gate.

Something cold settles in my stomach.

"Guys?" I take a step toward them. "What's—"

The bonds flare behind me. All six of them, humming with something I can't put my finger on.

Finn moves first, slipping his hand into mine. His chaos magic sparks against my skin — still brighter than before, still different — but there's something heavy in the way he's holding on.

Malrik appears at my other side. Steady. Silent.

Torric's heat presses against my back. Aspen's frost cools the air at my shoulder. Darian's light flickers soft and uncertain. Kieran's presence anchors the edges.

They're surrounding me.

Not protectively. Not like there's a threat.

Like they're bracing me for something.

"What's going on?" My voice comes out sharper than I mean it to. "Why are they just standing there? Why aren't they—"

"Kaia." Aspen's voice is quiet. Gentle in a way that makes my chest tight. "Look at them."

I am looking at them. That's the problem.

They're standing in a line like soldiers waiting for orders. Patricia's notebook is *closed*. Finnick hasn't moved in thirty seconds. And they keep looking between me and the Gate. Back and forth. Gate. Me. Gate. Me.

My mother's sisters-in-arms.

The Valkyries who fell that night and bound their souls to me through the Heart of Eternity. Who chose to stay when they could have passed on. Who protected me, guided me, loved me — for *centuries* — waiting for this moment.

For me to open the Gate.

"They've been waiting for you," Torric says softly. His hand lands on my shoulder. Warm. Heavy. "Not the Gate."

I couldn't have done any of this without them. Not a single step. And now—

No.

No, I'm not thinking about that. Not yet.

"It is time."

The God's voice cuts through everything. He's beside me suddenly, quiet and inevitable, watching my shadows with an expression I can't read.

I know what he's going to say. I know it in my bones, in the way my chest is already cracking open.

I ask anyway.

"Time for what?"

He holds my gaze. Ancient. Gentle. Sorry.

"For them to go home."

"No." The word rips out of me before he's finished speaking. "No, not yet. I'm not ready."

The shadows don't move. A few of them lower their heads — patient, affectionate, waiting.

"They stayed for you," the God says softly. "Protected you. Guided you to your Gate. But they cannot remain. Not now that their purpose is fulfilled."

"Their purpose isn't—" My voice cracks. "They're my *family*."

My voice breaks on the word. Finn's hand tightens in mine.

"They always will be." The God's voice is impossibly gentle. "On the other side, memory does not fade. Service does not end. But here? They are trapped between worlds. Let them go home, Kaia."

I'm shaking.

I can feel it — the tremor running through my whole body, my wings, the bonds in my chest.

"I can't." Tears burn my eyes. "I can't just let them—"

Mouse moves.

He pads forward, massive and ancient, and presses his head against my palm. His fur is warm. Real. Solid in a way shadows shouldn't be.

Little one.

His voice slides into my mind — rare, sacred, heavy with centuries.

Not all of us are leaving.

I freeze.

"What?"

The one you call Walter and I are guardians. Bound to the Valkyrie line itself, not to individual souls. We stay.

The relief hits so hard my knees almost buckle.

"You're staying? You're not—"

We will never leave you, little one. Not until you no longer need us. And even then...

His violet eyes hold mine.

Even then, we will find a way.

A sob escapes me. I sink to my knees in the snow and wrap my arms around his massive neck, burying my face in shadow-fur that feels more real than anything.

"Thank you," I choke out. "Thank you, thank you—"

Mouse rumbles. A purr that vibrates through my chest.

But the others must go. They have waited centuries for this moment. For you to open the Gate. For you to release them.

I pull back. Wipe my face with shaking hands.

The others.

Bob. Patricia. Finnick. Carl. Steve. Linda.

They're still standing in their line, watching me with small movements I've never seen from them before.

It's hope.

"They want to go," I whisper.

They are tired, little one. They have served faithfully for so long. Let them rest.

I nod. I don't trust my voice.

Behind me, I feel my men shift closer. Finn's chaos sparking with grief he's trying to hide. Torric's fire banked to embers. Aspen's frost crackling with emotion. Malrik's shadow magic restless. Darian's light flickering. Kieran's presence heavy with understanding.

They feel it too.

They love them too.

Carl moves first.

Because of course he does. He's already halfway to the Gate before anyone realizes what's happening, then he stops, looks back like he forgot something important, and waves.

At me. At Torric. At a rock, for some reason.

His form flickers and I see him — quick, curious, mischief written into every line of his face. A scout. The kind of person who climbed things just to see what was up there and fell out of half of them.

He salutes — sloppy, cheerful, completely Carl — and then turns and sprints toward the Gate like it's a race nobody else knew they were running.

The light takes him.

Gone.

Steve tries to follow and immediately trips over his own feet.

He scrambles up, flickering into a young man with earnest eyes and a crooked smile. The kind of person who never stopped trying no matter how many times he failed.

He looks back at us, waves awkwardly, takes three steps, stumbles, catches himself, gives a thumbs up like he totally meant to do that.

Finn laughs. Wet and broken, but real.

Steve beams at him. Then he turns and walks into the light, only stumbling twice more on the way.

Gone.

Linda steps forward next.

She doesn't come to me first.

She goes to Aspen.

Her form flickers — a woman with kind eyes and steady hands, silver streaking through dark hair. The sort of person who held everything together when nothing else would.

She cups his face. Gentle. Maternal.

Aspen's frost crackles. His eyes are wet.

She smooths her thumb across his cheek, wiping away a tear he didn't notice falling. Then she presses a kiss to his forehead.

She moves to Torric next, smoothing down his hair like he's a kid who's been running wild. He ducks his head, embarrassed, but doesn't pull away.

To Finn and Malrik — wraps shadow-arms around both of them at once. Malrik's shoulders shake. Just once.

To Darian — he flinches, then melts into her touch. She strokes his hair until he stops trembling.

To Kieran — takes his hands, squeezes twice. A silent promise.

When she reaches me, she pulls me into a hug that feels like every comfort I've ever needed.

I break.

Completely. Sobbing into her shoulder, clinging to her like I can keep her here if I just hold on tight enough.

"I don't want you to go."

She strokes my hair. Rocks me gently. Presses a kiss to the top of my head.

Then she pulls back. Cups my face in shadow-hands. Wipes my tears with thumbs that feel real and solid and warm.

She points at me. Then at my chest. Then at the men surrounding us. She mimes a circle — all of us together.

Family, she's saying. *You have family. You're not alone.*

"I know," I whisper. "I know. Thank you. For taking care of all of us."

She smiles. Soft. Proud. Tired.

Then she walks toward the Gate.

I watch her go until the light swallows her whole.

Finnick bounces forward next — and even now, even in this moment, he can't help himself.

He does a flip. A dramatic bow. Jazz hands that shouldn't be possible for a shadow.

His form flickers, and I see him — young, wild-eyed, a chaos mage with a grin that could start wars. He looks exactly like Finn. *Exactly.* Same auburn hair. Same green eyes. Same mischief written into every line of his face.

Finn makes a choked sound beside me.

"Hey." His voice is wrecked. "That's— you look like— you little shit, were you mocking me this whole time?"

Finnick's grin widens. He points at Finn, then at himself, then does that stupid little flip thing that Finn does when he's showing off.

Then he darts forward and hugs Finn — shadow arms wrapping around him, squeezing tight.

Finn breaks. Just completely shatters, holding onto a shadow like it's the only thing keeping him upright.

Finnick pulls back. Cups Finn's face in shadow-hands. Goes suddenly serious. Ancient. *Knowing.*

He points at Finn's chest. At his heart. Then at me.

Take care of her.

Finn nods, tears streaming. "I will. I swear."

Finnick grins again — bright, mischievous, *alive* — pats Finn's cheek, boops his nose, and cartwheels toward the Gate.

One final flip at the threshold. Peace sign.

Gone.

Finn's knees buckle. Malrik catches him, pulls him close, holds him up.

Patricia steps forward.

She's calm. Composed. Of course she is.

Her form flickers and I see her — young, fierce, ink-stained fingers and sharp eyes. Not the quiet scholar I imagined. A warrior in her own right.

She holds out her notebook.

I take it with trembling hands. It's heavier than it looks. Warmer.

She taps the cover. Taps her heart. Gestures at all of us.

Remember. I remembered for you. Now it's yours.

She looks at the guys — one long sweep that catalogs all of them one final time. Then she points at me, points at them, and mimes something that's very clearly a threat. Finger across throat. Pointing at each of them.

Finn laughs, wet and broken. "Yeah, we get it. Take care of her or else."

Patricia nods. Satisfied.

She doesn't hug me. That's not who she is. Instead, she places her hand over my heart, holds it there for a moment, and nods once.

You did well.

Then she walks into the light.

Bob is last.

He steps forward, and for the first time since I've known him, his edges soften. His rigid posture eases.

His form flickers and I see him.

Tall. Scarred. Commander's posture worn into his bones. Gray at his temples, lines around his eyes. A face that's seen centuries of war and kept standing anyway.

He served my mother.

I don't know how I know that, but I do. I feel it somewhere deep. He was there. He watched her fall. He's been waiting ever since.

He stops in front of Torric first.

Torric goes rigid. His fire flares, then banks. His jaw does that thing where he's trying really hard not to feel anything.

Bob clasps his arm. Warrior to warrior. Something passes between them that doesn't need words.

Torric nods. Sharp. Military.

Bob moves to Aspen — grips his shoulder, squeezes once. To Finn — hesitates, then pulls him into a hug that makes Finn sob harder against Malrik's chest. To Malrik — clasps his hand while Malrik's shadow magic reaches toward him like it's trying to hold on. To Darian — places a hand over his heart, holds it there. To Kieran — bows, ancient to ancient, two soldiers who've seen too much.

Then he comes to me.

He stops. Stands at attention. Perfect form. Perfect stillness.

And then — slowly, carefully — he reaches out and takes my hand.

His grip is firm. Solid. Real.

He places my hand over his heart. Holds it there.

I can feel it. The centuries of service. The loyalty. The love.

"Commander Bob." My voice is wrecked. Shattered. "Thank you. For staying. For protecting me. For—" I can't finish. Can't find words big enough.

He squeezes my hand once.

Then he steps back.

Salutes.

Perfect. Crisp. The salute he's been saving for this moment. For me.

I salute back. Sloppy. Tearful. The worst salute in the history of salutes.

But his form ripples. Something that might be a smile.

He holds it for one more moment.

Then he turns and walks toward the Gate.

He doesn't look back.

The light swallows him.

And he's gone.

Walter drifts forward.

He hovers in front of me, pulsing that strange violet light, and I feel something pass between us.

Not words. Not images. Just understanding.

He's staying.

He pulses once — bright, warm, proud — and then drifts back to hover at my shoulder.

Where he's always been.

Where he'll always be.

Mouse pads forward and sits at my feet.

It is done, he says into my mind. *They are home.*

I look at the Gate.

Still glowing. Still humming. But different now. Lighter, somehow. Like a weight has been lifted.

Bob. Patricia. Finnick. Carl. Steve. Linda.

Gone.

After centuries of waiting, of protecting, of serving — they're finally home.

And I'm the one who got to send them there.

I collapse.

My knees hit the snow and I'm falling forward, and there are arms around me.

They hold me while I break.

Finn is crying too. I can feel his tears on my shoulder, his chaos magic sparking with grief. Malrik's arms are shaking. Torric's fire keeps flaring and banking like he can't control it. Aspen's frost is spreading across the snow around us. Darian's light flickers like a candle in wind. Kieran's composure has cracked — I can feel it through the bond, the grief he's trying to hide and failing.

We're all breaking.

All of us.

Together.

"You honored them well, Valkyrie."

The God's voice is soft. Distant.

I can't respond. Can barely breathe.

But Mouse presses against my side, warm and solid and here.

Walter pulses above me, violet and bright and staying.

And somewhere underneath the grief, underneath the loss—

Peace.

They're home.

I'm so lucky to have been the one to give them that.

Chapter 6
ASPEN

It's too quiet.

The kind of quiet that comes after something massive has passed through and left emptiness in its wake.

No shuffling Eds. No shadow army stretching to the horizon. Just wind and snow and the Gate humming soft behind us, and the seven of us tangled together in the aftermath.

Kaia is on her knees in the snow, wings drooping, feathers trailing in the white. Still crying, but quieter now — the exhausted kind of tears that come when you've already broken and there's nothing left to shatter.

I'm behind her, one hand on her neck, feeling her pulse race beneath my fingers. Finn is pressed against her left side, face buried in her shoulder, Malrik's arms wrapped around both of them. Torric is at her back, fire banked so low I can barely feel his heat. Darian hovers at the edge, light flickering, one hand half-raised like he wants to reach for her but isn't sure he's allowed. Kieran kneels a few feet away — close, but not touching. Not yet.

Mouse sits at Kaia's feet, solid and warm.

Walter pulses at her shoulder, violet and bright.

That's it.

That's all that's left.

I breathe in. Cold air, thin and sharp. My frost rises to meet the quiet responding the way it always does when my emotions run too deep to speak.

I've learned to read this group over the past months. The way Finn's jokes get sharper when he's scared. The way Malrik's control tightens right before it breaks.

Right now, everyone is breaking. Quietly. Together.

Kaia's breath hitches under my palm. I smooth my thumb across the back of her neck, a small grounding touch.

"Breathe," I murmur. Just for her. "We've got you."

She doesn't respond, but she leans back into my hand. Just slightly.

The wind picks up. Snow swirls around us. Somewhere far below, in the valley, I catch the faint smell of earth instead of ash. The realm already healing.

I don't know how long we stay like that. Minutes. Maybe longer. Time feels strange right now, stretched thin and fragile.

Then the air shifts.

I feel it before I see it — a pressure change, a weight settling into the space beside us.

The God of Chaos.

He doesn't announce himself. Doesn't appear in a flash of light or a crack of thunder. He's just *there*, standing a few feet away, watching us with those endless eyes.

I'm the first to notice. I lift my head, meet his gaze.

He inclines his head slightly.

"You honored them well," he says. His voice is quiet. Gentle in a way that doesn't match what he is. "All of you."

Torric's fire flares. Finn makes a sound against Kaia's shoulder — not quite a laugh, not quite a sob. Malrik's grip tightens on both of them. Darian's light steadies for a moment, then flickers again.

Kaia doesn't move. I don't think she can.

The God's gaze sweeps across our group.

Then his eyes find mine.

"The steady one," he says. Not a question. "The calm at the center of the storm."

I don't know how to respond to that. I'm not calm. I'm holding on by my fingernails, frost crackling under my skin, grief sitting heavy in my chest.

But I understand what he means.

Someone has to stay standing when everyone else falls. Someone has to notice the cracks before they become chasms. Someone has to hold the line.

That's me. That's always been me.

"She needs time," I say quietly. "They all do."

"Yes." The God moves closer. Not threatening — just present. "And you will give it to them. That is your gift, Aspen. You see what others miss. You hold what others cannot."

My rune pulses cold against my arm.

He reaches into nothing — his hand disappears into empty air and comes back holding something small. A stone. Dark, about the size of my palm, with faint glowing veins running through it like frozen lightning.

He holds it out to me.

"When you are ready to return to your academy," he says, "this will take you home."

I take it. It's warm despite looking like volcanic glass. Heavier than it should be.

"Why me?"

"Because you will not use it before she is ready." His eyes flick to Torric, then back to me. "Others might. You will wait."

Fair. Torric would absolutely activate this thing the second he thought Kaia needed to leave.

I pocket the stone. Feel its weight settle against my thigh.

"Thank you."

The God nods. Then he moves past me, toward Kaia.

She's still on her knees. Still crying those quiet, exhausted tears. She looks smaller than I've ever seen her.

"Little Valkyrie."

His voice is impossibly soft. Kaia lifts her head slowly, like it weighs more than she can carry.

Her face is wrecked — red-eyed, tear-streaked, grief written into every line. She doesn't try to hide it. Doesn't have the energy.

"What now?" Her voice is hoarse. Broken. "What am I supposed to do now?"

The God crouches in front of her. Puts himself at her level instead of towering over her.

"Now," he says, "you rest. You heal. You let them—" he gestures at all of us, "—carry you for a while."

"I don't know how to do that."

"You will learn." He reaches out, almost touches her face, then stops. Pulls back. "You restored something today that has been broken for centuries. You returned souls to their rest. You opened a Gate that would have stayed closed forever, and you did it with love instead of force."

Kaia's breath catches.

"The next part is not mine to guide," the God continues. "What comes after the war is always harder than the war itself. But you are not alone. You have never been alone."

He looks at Kieran then. Direct. Pointed.

Kieran's jaw tightens. His fingers tremble once before he forces them still.

"Centuries of regret," the God says quietly. "Centuries of punishment you inflicted on yourself. Tonight, let it rest. She carries your absolution now. Has carried it longer than you've been willing to accept."

Kieran's composure cracks. I see it — the fissure running through that ancient stillness, the way his breath goes sharp and uneven.

Kaia reaches for him.

It's instinctive. Unconscious. Her hand stretches out, and Kieran moves like he's been waiting centuries for permission.

He catches her hand. Pulls her into his arms. Holds her like she's the only thing keeping him tethered to the world.

The bonds flare. All of them, all at once — grief and love and something that feels like healing.

Kaia buries her face in Kieran's chest. His hand comes up to cradle the back of her head, fingers tangling in her hair.

The God watches them for a moment. Then he stands.

"Heal," he says to all of us. "Rest. Love each other. Return when you are ready — not before."

He looks at each of us in turn. Finn, still crying against Malrik. Torric, fire finally steadying. Darian, whose light finally evens out as he watches Kaia in Kieran's arms. Me, with the stone heavy in my pocket.

Kieran and Kaia, wrapped around each other like they're afraid to let go.

"You will see me again," the God says. "But not soon. Not until it is time."

He tilts his head, studying us with something that might be fondness.

"You cannot heal on a frozen plateau. Let me give you one last gift."

He snaps his fingers.

Light flares — bright, warm, gentle — and the world *shifts*.

When my vision clears, we're not on the plateau anymore.

We're in Japti.

The great hall stretches around us, familiar and impossible. Warm light glows from the walls. The air smells like stone and fire and something ancient. The six bloodline halls branch off in their circle — and at the center, next to the hot spring, soft furs and cushions have been arranged like someone knew we were coming.

Which, I suppose, someone did.

The God stands at the edge of the hall, already fading.

"Rest," he says again. "You've earned it."

And then he's gone.

The silence that follows is different. Softer. Warmer.

Mouse pads over to me. Sits at my feet. Looks up with those ancient violet eyes.

They will need time, his voice slides into my mind. *But they have it now. Thanks to her.*

Walter drifts closer, pulses once — warm, reassuring — and settles at my shoulder.

A weight I hadn't realized I was carrying unspools from my chest.

We're not alone. Even with Bob and Patricia and Finnick and Linda and Steve and Carl gone — we're not alone.

I look at my family.

Kaia and Kieran, still tangled together, centuries of hurt finally cracking open. Finn and Malrik, holding each other through grief that's turning into something else. Torric, fire steady now, watching Kaia with that fierce protective love he doesn't know how to hide. Darian, light finally calm, one hand pressed to his chest like he's holding something precious in place.

We're broken. All of us, in different ways.

But we're together.

I touch the stone in my pocket. Feel its warmth against my palm.

Not yet.

Not because the God commanded it — but because none of us are ready to face the world again.

Before we return to the academy, before we figure out what comes next—

We need each other first.

Chapter 7
KIERAN

I've been awake for hours.

Maybe longer. Time moves strangely in Japti — the light never quite changes, the air stays warm and still, and I've lost track of how many times we've slept and woken and slept again.

Days. Its been days since the Gate. Since the shadows passed through. Since she collapsed in my arms and I carried her here, to the furs by the hot spring, and held her while she cried herself unconscious.

She's still asleep.

Curled against my chest, her breath warm and slow against my throat. Her face is softer in sleep — the grief lines smoothed out, the tension in her jaw finally eased.

She's been cycling between crying and unconscious for what feels like an eternity. Last night — or what passed for last night — we bathed her in the hot spring. All of us. Gentle hands washing blood and ash from her skin, removing the salt from her hair, holding her steady when her legs gave out.

She fell asleep before I finished rinsing her hair.

I carried her to the furs. Wrapped her in warmth. Held her while the others settled around us in a protective circle.

And now I can't move.

Not because I'm injured. Not because I'm trapped.

Because I'm terrified that if I let go, she'll vanish again.

The way she did centuries ago. The way I've dreamed about for hundreds of years — when we finally made it to the Valkyries that night and I couldn't find her, leaving me alone with the weight of everything I couldn't stop.

Even now, unconscious, she twitches. Restless. Running from something in her dreams.

I smooth my hand down her spine. A slow, steady stroke.

"Shh," I murmur. "I'm here. You're safe."

She settles. Just barely. Her fingers curl tighter into my shirt.

I don't move.

I hardly breathe.

I just hold her.

The others are already awake.

I hear them moving quietly at the edges of my awareness.

They're giving us space.

I don't know when they left. Don't know what silent agreement passed between them. But one by one, they slipped away — Finn and Malrik first, whispering something I didn't catch. Torric gesturing toward the Valkyrie hall before disappearing into its shadows. Darian going silently, without looking back.

Aspen was last.

He paused at the edge of the furs, looked at me with those ice-blue eyes that see too much, and nodded once.

You need this. She needs this. We're giving you space.

Then he was gone.

And it's just us.

Kaia and me.

The bond hums between us — warm and golden and finally, *finally* free of the guilt I deserve. No more walls. No more distance. Just her, nestled against my chest, and me, holding on like I'll die if I let go.

My dragon stirs.

Ours, he rumbles, then settles back. Content to watch. To wait.

I close my eyes.

Yes. Finally.

She stirs.

At first I think it's another nightmare — another restless twitch, another whimper I'll soothe with my hands and my voice.

But then she shifts against me. Really shifts. Her breath changes — deeper, slower, the rhythm of someone surfacing from sleep.

Her fingers uncurl from my shirt. Curl again. Like she's checking that I'm real.

"Kieran…"

My entire body goes still.

Her voice is soft. Muzzy with sleep. But she said my name. *My name.*

"I'm here." The words come out rougher than I intend. "I'm right here."

She makes a sound — something between a sigh and a hum — and nuzzles closer. Her lips brush my throat. Warm. Soft.

"My dragon…"

My heart stops.

"My oldest love…"

I can't breathe. Can't think. Can't do anything but lie perfectly still while she mumbles against my skin, half-asleep and completely destroying me.

"I remember you," she whispers. "From back then…"

Back then.

The field. The first time she touched my scales and something *zipped* through both of us — recognition, belonging, the bone-deep knowledge that we were connected in ways neither of us understood.

She was six years old. I was just a boy, finally able to shift. And she looked up at my dragon form with those violet eyes and said *pretty* like it was the most obvious thing in the world.

I've never recovered.

"The field," she murmurs now, still groggy, still half-dreaming. "Your beautiful dragon…"

My hand trembles against her back.

"The way something zipped through me when I touched your scales…"

She tilts her head, presses a sleepy kiss to the underside of my jaw.

"It felt like you were mine."

I break.

Everything in me — dragon and man, ancient and new, all the centuries of waiting and wanting and *aching* — bows to that.

"I am yours, Kaia." The words tear out of me, hoarse and desperate. "Every part of me. My body. My dragon. My past and my future." I cup the back of her head, press my forehead to hers. "Then, now… always."

She sighs. Soft and warm and *content.*

Then she snuggles closer and kisses my neck.

Not sleepy this time.

Deliberate.

Her teeth graze my pulse point and I shudder.

Fully awake now. Fully here. Fully aware of what she's doing as her lips trace up my throat, as her tongue flicks against the sensitive spot beneath my ear, as her fingers slide under my shirt to rake across my chest.

She pulls back just enough to look at me. Her eyes clear. Violet eyes dark with want, sharp with certainty.

Then she pulls me down into a kiss.

Not tentative. Not asking permission.

Claiming.

I give her everything. My mouth opens against hers, and she makes a sound — a small, desperate sound that goes straight to my cock. Her tongue slides against mine and I'm already hard, already aching, already lost.

"Please," she whispers against my lips. "I need you. I've needed you for so long and I didn't even know—"

I roll her onto her back.

The furs slip down and she's bare beneath them — golden skin warm from sleep, from the bath we gave her last night. I've seen her naked before, but not like this. Not spread out beneath me with that look in her eyes, the one that says *take me.*

"Gods, Kaia." I pull back just to look at her. Golden hair spread across dark fur. Flushed cheeks. Parted lips. The soft swell of her breasts rising and falling with each shallow breath. "You're so beautiful it hurts."

"Then stop looking." She reaches for me. "And touch me."

I lower my mouth to her throat.

She gasps when my lips find her pulse. Moans when I suck gently, tasting the salt of her skin. Her hands fly to my hair, fingers tangling, pulling me closer.

"Centuries," I murmur against her skin. "I've waited centuries for you."

"I know." Her voice breaks. "I'm sorry it took me so long to remember."

"Don't." I kiss lower. The ridge of her collarbone. The hollow between her breasts. "Don't apologize. That's mine to do. You're here now. We're here now. That's what matters."

I take my time.

I've waited too long to rush this.

My mouth traces the curve of her breast, and she arches into me, a whimper escaping her lips. I circle her nipple with my tongue — slow, teasing — and she makes a sound that's almost a sob.

"Kieran—"

I draw her into my mouth and suck.

Her whole body jerks. Her fingers tighten in my hair until it hurts, and I groan against her skin, the pain only making me harder.

I lavish attention on one breast, then the other. Licking. Sucking. Grazing with my teeth until she's writhing beneath me, her hips rolling up against nothing, desperate for friction.

"Please," she gasps. "Please, I need—"

"I know what you need."

I kiss down her stomach. Dip my tongue into her navel just to hear her gasp. Press my lips to the soft skin of her hip, the crease where her thigh meets her body.

She's shaking by the time I settle between her legs.

I look up at her. Hold her gaze as I press a kiss to the inside of her thigh. Then the other. Then higher, close enough that she can feel my breath on her core.

"Kieran." Her voice is wrecked. "Please. Stop teasing."

"Never." I press another kiss, just beside where she wants me. "I've waited centuries for this. I'm going to savor every second."

"I'm going to *kill* you—"

I lick her.

One long, slow stroke from her entrance to her clit, and she screams.

Her thighs clamp around my head. Her hips buck up off the furs. Her hands twist in my hair so hard I see stars.

I don't stop.

I learn her with my tongue — every fold, every secret spot, every place that makes her gasp and shake. She tastes like heaven. Like everything I've been denied for hundreds of years finally given to me.

I circle her clit with the tip of my tongue and she sobs my name. I seal my lips around it and suck, and her whole body arches like a bow.

"Oh gods— Kieran— I can't— I'm going to—"

I slide two fingers inside her.

She's so wet, so ready, that they slip in easily. I curl them, searching, and find the spot that makes her shatter.

She comes on my tongue.

Her thighs shake. Her hands pull my hair. She cries out my name like a prayer, like a curse, like something sacred and profane all at once.

I work her through it, licking and stroking until the aftershocks fade and she's lying boneless beneath me, chest heaving.

"Gods," she breathes. "That was... I..."

I press a kiss to her inner thigh. Slide my fingers out of her slowly, watching her shiver at the loss.

"We're not done."

Her eyes widen.

I crawl up her body, kissing her stomach, her breasts, her throat. She tastes herself on my lips when I kiss her and moans into my mouth.

"I need you inside me," she whispers against my lips. "Please, Kieran. I need to feel you."

I reach down and strip off my pants. Kick them away. When I settle back over her, the head of my cock presses against her entrance, and we both groan.

Her arms lift. Instinctive. Wrists crossing above her head.

I freeze.

"Kaia—"

"Hold me there." Her voice is soft but certain. "I want you to hold me there. I want to feel you everywhere. I want to give you everything."

Something breaks open in my chest.

I reach up. Wrap my fingers around both her wrists. Pin them gently but firmly to the furs above her head.

She arches into me immediately — a full-body shiver, her breath catching, her pupils blowing wide.

"Yes," she breathes. "Like that. Just like that."

I hold her there. Let her feel the weight of my grip. Let her feel how much I want this — how much I've always wanted this.

"Look at me," I murmur.

She does. Violet eyes dark with need, lips swollen from my kisses, cheeks flushed with pleasure.

"I love you." The words come easier than I expected. Maybe because I've been holding them for centuries. "I have loved you since you were a child looking up at my dragon like I was something beautiful instead of something terrifying. I have loved you through time and death and realms. I will love you until the stars burn out and the gods forget their names."

Tears slip down her temples.

"Kieran—"

I push into her.

Slow. Inch by inch. Giving her time to adjust to the size of me, the stretch.

Her head falls back, mouth open on a silent cry. Her wrists strain against my grip. Her legs fall open wider, welcoming me deeper.

"You feel—" She can't finish. Can't form words. "*Kieran.*"

I seat myself fully inside her and hold still.

She's so tight. So warm. So *perfect* that I have to close my eyes and breathe through the urge to come right now.

"I can feel you," she gasps. "Through the bond — I can feel everything you're feeling—"

"I know." I press deeper, impossibly deeper, and she moans. "I feel it too. Everything. Your pleasure. Your need. Your love."

I start to move.

Slow at first. Long, deep strokes that drag against every sensitive spot inside her. She whimpers with each one, her hips trying to roll up to meet me, her wrists pulling against my grip.

"More," she breathes. "Please, Kieran. I need more."

"Tell me what you need."

"Harder." She wraps her legs around my waist, heels digging into my back. "Faster. I need— I need—"

I give her what she needs.

The pace breaks. My control shatters.

I drive into her — hard, deep, relentless. She meets every thrust with a roll of her hips and a cry that echoes through the empty hall. The sound of our bodies coming together fills the space. Wet. Obscene. *Perfect*.

She pulls against my grip on her wrists — not to get free, just to feel it. Just to feel held. Just to feel *owned*.

"You're mine," I growl against her throat. "Say it."

"Yours." She can barely breathe. "Always — oh gods, *right there* — always yours."

I angle my hips to hit that spot again. Again. Again.

She screams.

"That's it." I'm losing myself. Losing everything except her, except this. "Let go for me, Kaia. I've got you. I'll always have you."

Her whole body tightens around me.

"Kieran— I'm— I can't—"

"Let go."

She shatters.

Her back arches off the furs. Her walls clamp down on my cock so hard I can barely breathe. She cries out my name — broken, beautiful, *mine* — and the bond blazes between us, golden light flooding through both of us.

I feel everything she feels. Every wave of pleasure. Every pulse of release. Every ounce of love she has for me reflected back through the bond.

It destroys me.

I bury myself deep and come so hard my vision whites out. Her name tears from my throat like a prayer. I spill into her in waves, centuries of longing cresting and breaking and flooding through me until I'm empty and full all at once.

We stay like that.

Tangled together. Trembling. Breathing.

I release her wrists, and she immediately wraps her arms around my neck, pulling me down against her. I bury my face in her hair. Breathe her in.

Her fingers stroke through my hair. Gentle. Loving.

"Centuries," she whispers. "You waited centuries for me."

I lift my head. Meet her eyes.

"I would have waited longer."

She pulls me down into a kiss. Soft. Slow. The kind of kiss that says *I know*. The kind of kiss that says *me too*.

When we break apart, she's crying again. But these tears are different — warm and quiet, sliding down her temples into her hair.

"I never forgot you," she says. "Not really. Even before I knew your name... I remembered your dragon. The way you made me feel safe."

I gather her against my chest. Press my face into her hair. Hold her so tight I'm not sure where I end and she begins.

"You are safe," I murmur. "Always. I swear it."

Her breathing slows. Her body relaxes into mine.

She falls asleep between one breath and the next.

I don't follow. Not yet.

Instead, I hold her. Watch the soft rise and fall of her chest. Feel the bond humming warm and steady between us, brighter than it's ever been.

Centuries.

I've waited centuries for this.

And now that I have her — now that she's here, in my arms, remembering me the way I've always remembered her—

I'm never letting go.

Chapter 8
TORRIC

The Valkyrie hall is quiet when I push through the archway.

Kieran and Kaia are tangled together in the furs near the fire. Her head tucked against his chest. His arms wrapped around her like he's afraid she'll dissolve if he lets go.

She's breathing slow. Deep. Peaceful.

For the first time in days — maybe weeks — she's actually *resting*.

I stop a few feet away. Let myself look.

Kieran's eyes are open. He meets my gaze over her head, and something passes between us.

Relief.

He nods once. I nod back.

Movement behind me. The others filing in. Aspen first, settling against the wall near the entrance. Darian a moment later, keeping his distance, that faint glow leaking from him the way it does when his emotions are running high. Malrik next, eyes red and worn, shoulders carrying too much. And Finn trailing behind him, already opening his mouth to say something stupid.

They spread out around the fire pit — close enough to talk, far enough to give Kieran and Kaia space.

Mouse is curled at the foot of the furs, tail wrapped around his paws. Walter bobs lazily near the ceiling, pulsing that faint violet light.

Finn's mouth opens.

"Don't," Kieran says quietly.

"I didn't say anything."

"You were about to."

"You don't know that."

"I've known you for months. I absolutely know that."

Finn's grin spreads across his face. "Fine. I was going to say you look comfortable. Centuries of waiting and you finally got the girl. Literally. She's on top of you."

"She's beside me."

"Semantics."

Kieran's mouth twitches. Then he shifts carefully, one hand sliding beneath Kaia's head to support it as he extracts himself from the furs. She makes a soft sound of protest, fingers curling into the blanket where his shirt used to be, but she doesn't wake.

He freezes. We all freeze.

She settles. Sighs. Burrows deeper into the warmth he left behind.

Kieran exhales slowly and finishes extricating himself. He tucks the furs around her, brushes hair from her face, then stands and joins us by the fire.

He moves stiffly. Like his body hasn't caught up with the fact that he's allowed to relax now.

"She's really out," Finn says.

"She earned it." Kieran lowers himself onto one of the stone benches, close enough to reach her if she stirs. "She's been running on nothing for weeks."

"We all have." Malrik is sitting across the fire, and gods, he looks wrecked. Whatever happened while Kieran and Kaia were in here hit him hard.

"But her especially." Kieran's gaze stays on her face. "The Gate. The shadows leaving. The God. She carried all of it."

The words land heavy.

Because he's right.

Bob. Patricia. Finnick. Linda. Steve. Carl. Gone. Passed through the Gate. Finally home.

I watched them go. Watched Kaia break apart saying goodbye. Watched Bob give her that final salute and walk into the light without looking back.

My chest still hurts.

"She loved them," Aspen says. "Like family."

"They *were* family. They'd been with her since before she was born." Kieran's voice is rough. "Bob served her mother for three hundred years. Patricia documented every major event in Valkyrie history. Linda helped raise Kaia when she was small."

"You knew them," Malrik says. Not a question.

"I knew all of them. I met them the few times I was lucky enough to travel with my father. Before.. everything." He pauses. "And now they're home."

Walter pulses softly. Mouse's tail twitches once.

Not all of them left.

"She still has Mouse," Finn says. "And Walter. And us."

"She has us." Kieran's arm rests on his knee, his body angled toward her even now. "She'll always have us."

The fire crackles. Silence stretches.

Then Finn, because he can't help himself: "So. We should probably acknowledge the elephant in the room."

"What elephant?" Darian asks.

"The fact that we all heard everything."

Kieran goes very still.

"These walls aren't exactly thick," Finn continues, gesturing at the stone around us. "And she was... enthusiastic."

"Finn," Malrik warns.

"What? I'm not saying it's bad. I'm saying we all know what happened. We felt it through the bond. We heard it through the stone and wood. Pretending otherwise is stupid."

Kieran's jaw works. "And your point?"

"My point is—" Finn spreads his hands. "Good for you, man. Seriously. Centuries of pining and you finally—"

"I did not *pine*."

"You absolutely pined. You brooded and lurked and watched from doorways like a sad golden-eyed gargoyle."

"Dragon. And I was protecting her."

"From behind pillars. While she was with other men. Very protective."

Malrik snorts. I can't help it — I do too.

Kieran's eyes narrow. "I am capable of watching over her safety while she's otherwise occupied."

"Uh huh. And the watching had nothing to do with wanting to be the one she was occupied with?"

Silence.

Kieran doesn't answer.

"That's what I thought." Finn leans back, satisfied. "You're a voyeur, Kieran. Just admit it. It's fine. We've all got our things."

"I am not a—"

Rule #68 — if you're going to call an ancient dragon a voyeur to his face, make sure he's too exhausted to retaliate. Or that you can run faster than dragonfire.

"You watched me and Malrik in the hot spring. You tried to watch Torric and Kaia through the wall. You were at the cave entrance during Darian's—"

"I was standing *guard*."

"You were *watching*."

"Those are not mutually exclusive."

"So you admit it!"

Kieran pinches the bridge of his nose. "I admit nothing."

"Your silence speaks volumes."

"My silence is the only thing keeping me from throwing you into the fire."

"See, that's the thing though." Finn grins. "You won't. Because then Kaia would be sad. And you'd rather die than make her sad. So I get to mock you forever."

Kieran stares at him for a long moment.

Then his mouth curves. Just barely. "You are insufferable."

"I'm delightful."

"Those *are* mutually exclusive."

"They really aren't."

The tension breaks. Malrik shakes his head, but he's almost smiling. Aspen makes a sound that might be a laugh. Even Darian's shoulders have loosened.

This. Right here.

This is what we almost lost.

"She was happy," Darian says quietly. Almost to himself.

We all look at him.

He flushes. "I mean — through the bond. What I felt from her. She was..." He trails off, searching for the word. "Safe. For the first time in weeks. Really safe."

Kieran's expression softens. "She was."

"That's what matters, right?" Finn's voice has lost its teasing edge. "Not who she's with or what she's doing. Just that she's okay."

"She's more than okay," I say. "She's sleeping. Actually sleeping. Not passing out from exhaustion or crashing after a crisis. Sleeping. Because she feels safe enough to let go."

We all look at her.

Curled in the furs. Breathing steady. That small smile still on her lips. *Safe.*

When was the last time she felt that? Before the academy, probably. Before her power awakened. Before everything started hunting her.

"So." Finn stretches his legs out. "What now?"

Not a question about strategy. A life question.

"Wherever she wants," Kieran says immediately. "I've waited centuries. I can wait a little longer for her to decide."

"And if she decides to stay in Japti forever?" Darian asks.

"Then I stay in Japti forever."

"The academy?"

"Then I go back."

Finn leans forward, grinning. "A boat?"

Kieran blinks. "A boat?"

"I'm testing your commitment."

"Finn, I would follow her into the void itself. A boat is not a challenge."

"I'm just saying, you don't seem like a boat person."

"I have no strong feelings about boats."

"That's exactly what a non-boat person would say."

Kieran opens his mouth, closes it, and visibly decides not to engage.

"The point," Malrik cuts in, "is that we follow her lead. Wherever that takes us."

"Agreed," I say. "She's been pushed and pulled and controlled since she was a child. By Thorne. By Alekir. By the academy. By—" I look at Kieran.

He meets my gaze steadily. Waiting for it.

"By people who were supposed to protect her."

Kieran doesn't flinch. But something tightens in his jaw.

"She makes the choices now," I continue. "Where she goes. What she does. We're not her handlers. We're not her protectors deciding what's best for her behind her back."

"Even when she's wrong?" Darian asks.

"She's not ours to correct." I hold his gaze. "She's ours to stand beside."

Malrik leans forward, elbows on his knees. "We've all done it though. Made choices for her. Kept things from her. Told ourselves it was protection when really it was just... control we didn't want to name."

"I forced the bonds," Kieran interrupts quietly.

The fire pops.

"All of them. Without her consent. Without her knowledge. Because I was afraid of losing her again." His hands curl on his knees, knuckles white. "I told myself it was protection. Told myself she'd understand eventually. Told myself the end justified—" He stops. Swallows. "I was wrong. I don't get to make choices for her. Not ever again."

The admission sits between us. Heavy. Real.

Then Finn exhales loudly. "Well. That got dark."

"It was already dark," Aspen points out.

"Yeah, but we were doing the fun banter thing. I liked the fun banter thing."

"We can do both," Malrik says. "Acknowledge the heavy shit and still be idiots about it."

"That's... actually really healthy," Darian says. He sounds surprised.

"Don't get used to it."

"I won't."

Finn grins. "See, this is what I mean. We should be at each other's throats. Jealous and possessive and fighting over who gets to — I don't know — hold her hand or whatever. But instead we're just... this."

"This," Kieran repeats.

"Yeah. Whatever this is." Finn gestures vaguely at all of us. "She's sleeping over there after having sex with you, and instead of being weird about it, we're sitting here having a family meeting about vacation plans."

"We haven't discussed vacation plans."

"We should though. That's my point." Finn sits up straighter. "When was the last time any of us had a vacation? A real one? Not recovering from near-death. Not hiding from assassins. An actual, genuine, nothing-is-trying-to-kill-us vacation."

Silence.

Darian shakes his head. "Never."

"Same," Aspen says.

"Dragons don't take vacations," Kieran says.

"That's the saddest thing I've ever heard. You're how many years old and you've never had fun at a beach?"

"I've been to many beaches."

"For *fun*. Not for brooding purposes."

"There's nothing wrong with reflecting near the ocean."

"You just called it *reflecting*. That's just brooding with better PR."

"The waves are soothing."

"The waves are for *swimming*. And drinking. And making out with beautiful women. Not brooding — sorry, *reflecting*."

"I have made out with beautiful women at beaches."

Dead silence.

Every head turns toward Kieran.

His expression doesn't change, but there's something almost smug underneath it.

"*When?*" Finn demands.

"Centuries ago."

"How many centuries?"

"Several."

"That doesn't count!"

"It absolutely counts."

"You haven't kissed anyone in centuries and you think that qualifies as beach experience?"

"I've kissed Kaia."

"At a *beach*?"

"Not yet."

"Then it doesn't count!"

"When we reach the southern coast," Kieran says calmly, "I will kiss her at the beach. And then it will count."

Finn stares at him. "Did you just... make a future plan? A fun future plan? Not a battle strategy or a protection detail — an actual date?"

"I suppose I did."

"Who are you and what have you done with the brooding dragon?"

Kieran's mouth curves. "Perhaps I'm learning."

"From who? Certainly not from me. You never listen to me."

"I listen. I simply choose to ignore you."

"That's worse!"

The laughter that follows is real. Warm. The kind of sound I didn't know I needed until I heard it.

Even Kieran laughs. Small and rusty, like he's out of practice, but *there*. An actual laugh from the ancient bastard who spent centuries forgetting how.

Kaia shifts in the furs, mumbling something, and we all go quiet.

She settles. Doesn't wake. But her lips curve a little more.

"She's smiling," Darian says softly.

"She can feel us through the bond," Malrik says. "Even asleep. She knows we're here."

"What does she feel right now?" Finn asks. "Through the connection. What are we projecting?"

I reach for the bond. Try to identify the hum of it.

Warmth. Safety. Belonging. Something too big for a single word.

"Home," I say quietly. "She feels home."

The word sits there.

And something shifts. Not physically. Something in the bonds themselves. In what we've become.

"The southern coast," Kieran says after a moment. "Before the corruption. It was beautiful. White sand. Clear water. The kind of warmth that sinks into your bones and stays."

"You remember it?" Aspen asks.

"I remember everything." His voice goes soft. "It was one of her mother's favorite places. Solveig used to take Kaia there when she was small. Before. She'd chase the waves and Solveig would watch from the shore, and for a few hours everything was simple."

Something tightens in my chest.

Kaia doesn't remember her mother. Not really. Just fragments. Feelings. The ache of something missing.

But Kieran remembers.

"Then we take her there," I say. "When the realm heals. When she's ready."

"We make new memories," Malrik adds. "In the same place. Give her something good to hold onto."

"Vacation," Finn says dreamily. "Sand. Sun. Alcohol."

"Alcohol?" Aspen raises an eyebrow.

"I've earned it. We've all earned it. After the Gate and the shadows and the God and the—" He waves a hand. "Everything. I want to get drunk on a beach and not worry about anything trying to eat me."

"That's fair," Darian says.

"It's extremely fair."

"We'll need supplies," Malrik says, and there's something almost hopeful in his voice. Like he's letting himself think about a future that isn't just survival. "If we're actually doing this. Food. Shelter. Whatever passes for beach chairs in Absentia."

"Do beach chairs exist in Absentia?" Finn asks.

"They will when I'm done," Aspen says.

"Is that a threat or a promise?"

"Yes."

I laugh. Can't help it. The sound surprises me — rough and real, pulled from somewhere deep.

This. This is what we almost never got to have.

Kaia mumbles again in her sleep. Something that sounds like a name. Maybe several names.

We all go still. Watching.

She doesn't wake. Just sighs and settles deeper.

"She's dreaming," Kieran says softly. "I can feel it through the bond. It's... peaceful. For once."

"No nightmares?" Darian asks.

"No nightmares."

"Good."

The fire crackles. The silence is comfortable now. Warm.

"Family," Finn says after a while. Testing the word. "That's what this is, right? Some weird, dysfunctional, complicated—"

"Family," Kieran agrees. No hesitation.

Finn stops short. Stares at him.

"Did you just... agree with me? Without arguing?"

"You weren't wrong." Kieran's gaze moves across all of us. Something ancient and guarded finally unlocking in his expression. "I've spent centuries alone. Watching from the edges. Convincing myself I didn't need — that I couldn't have—" He stops. His jaw works. "This is family. The first one I've had since my father died. The first one I've let myself want."

The words land heavy.

Finn's expression does something complicated. For once, he doesn't joke.

"I didn't have one either," he says quietly. "Not really. Not one that wanted me."

"Same," Darian says. Almost inaudible.

"Mine was—" Malrik shakes his head. "Complicated. Broken in ways I'm still figuring out."

I think about our father. The man who beat us. Branded us. Tried to control what we'd become.

"Mine tried to destroy us," I say. "Made us into weapons instead of sons."

Aspen is quiet for a moment. Then: "We only had each other. Torric and me. After our sister... That was enough. But this—"

He looks around at all of us. At Kaia sleeping in the furs. At Mouse purring. At Walter pulsing soft violet near the ceiling.

"This is more," he finishes. "This is what family should have been."

Finn exhales shakily. "Well. Shit. We really are doing feelings around the campfire."

"You started it," Malrik points out.

"I know. I immediately regret it."

"No you don't."

"No. I don't." Finn scrubs a hand over his face. "This is — I don't know how to do this. The sincerity thing. It feels wrong coming out of my mouth."

"You're doing fine," Kieran says. Gentle, which is strange coming from him.

Finn laughs. Wet. Broken. "Great. The ancient dragon thinks I'm doing fine. My life is complete."

"It's a high compliment. I don't think most people are doing fine."

"What a glowing endorsement."

"Take what you can get."

Finn grins. It's shaky around the edges, but it's real. "Family, then. All of us. Even when we're idiots."

"Especially when we're idiots," Aspen says.

"Speak for yourself," Malrik mutters. "I'm never an idiot."

"You walked into a wall last week because you were watching Kaia."

"That wall was poorly placed."

"It was the same wall that's been there for centuries."

"Poorly. Placed."

Finn cackles. Darian chokes on a laugh. Even Kieran's mouth is twitching.

This. *This.*

I look around at all of them. These men I didn't choose. Didn't expect. Would die for without hesitation.

Family.

Brothers.

"She saved the world," I say after a while. Quiet. Certain. "Now we take care of her."

Kieran looks at Kaia. Watches her breathe.

"Always," he murmurs.

And I know he means it.

We all do.

Mouse purrs louder near her feet. Walter pulses warm.

The fire crackles.

And for the first time since this all started — maybe for the first time in my life — I feel like I'm exactly where I'm supposed to be.

Surrounded by brothers.

Watching over the woman who made us a family.

When she wakes… we follow her wherever she wants to go.

Chapter 9
KAIA

I wake up and nothing is trying to kill me.

That's... new.

No nightmare clawing its way up my throat. No bond screaming danger. No shadows bristling against threats I can't see yet.

No shadows...

I breathe deep.

Just warmth. Quiet. The soft crackle of fire and six bonds humming so low in my chest I almost mistake it for my own heartbeat.

Mouse is curled at my feet. Walter bobs near the ceiling, pulsing lazy violet.

I don't move.

I just... lie here. Like a person. Like someone who's allowed to exist without running.

When was the last time I did that?

The furs smell like Kieran. Smoke and pine and something old that I've stopped trying to put words to. I press my face into them like an idiot, and nobody's here to see it, so I let myself have this one stupid moment.

Three days. Give or take.

Three days of actual sleep. My body feels strange. Lighter. Like something that was wound too tight finally snapped loose.

Mouse lifts his head. Stares at me with those ancient eyes that have seen too much and judge accordingly.

Ready?

"Don't rush me," I mutter. "I just woke up."

His tail flicks. Judgment.

"Fine." I sit up. My spine cracks in three places. Rude. "I'm ready."

I find them on the other side of the cavern doing a terrible job of pretending they weren't waiting.

Kieran's sharpening a blade he doesn't need. Malrik and Aspen are arguing over a supply list that has maybe three items on it — none of which they agree on. Finn's eating something that's going to make him sick. Darian's holding a map upside down. Torric's leaning against the wall with his arms crossed, watching the doorway like—

Like he was waiting for me.

They all look up.

The bond hums. Warm. Steady. Annoying. Like someone stuffing comfort into my chest when I'm not ready for it.

Kieran stands. "You slept."

"Apparently." I stretch. Things pop. "How long was I out?"

"Three days," Finn says around a mouthful of whatever he's destroying. "We rounded up. You looked peaceful and none of us wanted to be the asshole who ruined it."

Malrik elbows him.

"What? It's true."

I laugh. It comes out rusty. Weird. Like my throat forgot how.

Then I take a breath. My chest tightens. My throat follows.

Complicated.

"It's time to go."

Silence.

Not the bad kind. Not the *Kaia's about to do something stupid* kind. Just... agreement. Like they were waiting for me to say it first.

Kieran nods. "Where?"

The question hits different now. Not *where's the threat* or *what's hunting us*. Just... where do I want to be?

My first real choice.

"The southern coast. The beach with the white sand and purple starfish that come near shore." I look at Kieran. "Where my mother used to take me."

Something shifts in his face. Soft. Aching. Old.

"I want to see it," I say. "I want to make new memories there. With—" I gesture vaguely at all of them. "You know. Everyone."

Smooth, Kaia. Very articulate.

Darian sets down his upside-down map. "I've never actually been to a beach."

Finn chokes. "Never?"

"The Light Faction wasn't known for leisure activities."

"That's genuinely tragic. That's the saddest thing I've heard today, and Kieran admitted he hasn't kissed anyone in centuries."

"I kissed Kaia three days ago."

"At a beach?"

"We've discussed this."

"Then it doesn't count!"

I snort. Can't help it.

Aspen, ever practical: "I can build seating. Chairs. Some kind of shade structure."

"I'm bringing alcohol," Finn announces. "Non-negotiable."

"Where are you getting alcohol?" Malrik asks.

"I'll figure it out. I'm resourceful."

"You're a disaster."

"A resourceful disaster. There's a difference."

Mouse winds between my ankles. Walter pulses warm overhead.

I look at them. These idiots. My idiots.

"The beach," I say. Certain. "Let's go."

We're gathering supplies — what little there is — when the air changes.

Something warm at my back. A glow I can feel before I see.

I turn.

The blank hall.

The one that's been nothing but stone and wood since we got here.

It's lighting up.

Golden threads weaving across the surface. Images forming. Moving.

"Kieran." My voice comes out weird. "What the hell is—"

He's beside me. His hand finds mine before I can pull away.

"Let's go see," he says quietly. "Whatever it is, it's for those who come after."

We all file in as the images keep forming.

And I realize what I'm looking at.

Us.

A little girl under a tree.

Golden hair. Shadows pooling around her like they're already hers. A small cat curled in her lap.

She's terrified. Crying. Lost. Nothing but a necklace and shadows in a world she doesn't know.

My chest cracks.

Because I remember this. The moment. The feeling.

"That's me," I whisper. "I was..."

The image shifts before I can finish.

The academy. Sharp and imposing against a gray sky.

A girl walks toward the gates. Shoulders tight. Trying to look like she's not terrified.

And on the roof — a figure with wild hair throws himself off the edge. Chaos magic sparking as he falls.

I choke on something between a laugh and a sob. "Finn."

"In my defense," he says behind me, "I stuck the landing."

"You almost broke your ankle."

"I stuck the *emotional* landing. You noticed me."

"I thought you were insane."

"Same thing."

An arena.

Three figures against a man. Another behind him, Thorne. Nightwraiths attacking.

And in the center — me. Terrified. Magic ripping out of me without permission.

Wings erupt from my back. Dark and light. Massive.

The first time.

Malrik inhales sharply. "I remember that."

"We all do," Darian says. Quiet.

I remember too. The fear. The power. The moment everything changed.

A doorway made of light.

Absentia on the other side. Beautiful and broken and impossible.

We step through together.

Monsters. Teeth. Things that shouldn't exist outside nightmares.

Torric and Aspen finding their berserker forms for the first time.

And then — fire. A dragon descending. Golden eyes blazing.

Kieran. Coming to rescue me.

"You came out of nowhere," I murmur.

His hand tightens on mine. "I was always there."

"Voyeur," Finn coughs.

"I will end you."

A library. Light through the windows.

Aspen. Ice-blue eyes. Frost on his fingertips.

The first time the bond felt gentle instead of violent.

I feel him step closer. Cool presence at my back.

A lake. Steam rising.

Malrik. Silver eyes. Kissing me like drowning. Like air.

I don't look at him. Don't need to. The bond says enough.

A village. Fire in a hearth.

Torric. Finally touching me without holding back.

My chest does something stupid.

Even my shadows lined up on the headboard.

Japti. The same sacred space.

Finn. All that chaos settling into something real.

A cave. Darkness.

Darian kneeling at my feet.

Broken. Trying. Earning it inch by inch.

The Gate.

Light pouring through. The God emerging. Alekir's end.

Me at the center. Wings spread. The Eds.

Bob's salute.

Patricia's notebook.

Finnick's bow.

Linda's final touch.

Walking into the light.

Going home.

My eyes burn. I blink hard. Don't cry. Don't—

Shit.

The image shifts one last time.

Us. Right now. Right here.

Standing in the hall. Six men behind one woman. Shadows at her feet.

And in the image — the painted version of this exact moment — I'm holding something.

A journal.

My breath stops.

I reach into my pack before I fully decide to. Fingers finding leather. Warm. It's always warm.

I pull it out.

The wall glows brighter. The image solidifies. Me. The journal. The final frame.

"Open it," Kieran says.

My hands are shaking. That's annoying.

I open it anyway.

Patricia's handwriting. Neat. Precise. I'd know it anywhere.

But this isn't notes. Isn't records.

A title.

Shadows of Change

By Patricia for my Kaia

I can't breathe.

The next page.

The end is only where we choose to rest. And Kaia? You have so much left to live.

The sob rips out of me. Ugly. Loud. Helpless.

My knees buckle.

Arms catch me. Warm hands. Familiar scents. The weight of six bonds anchoring me in place. Kieran at my back. Finn at my side. Hands everywhere. Holding me up.

"She wrote it," I manage. "She knew she was leaving and she still—"

"She loved you." Kieran's voice cracks. "They all did."

I press the journal to my chest. Leather and ink and something that still smells like her.

For my Kaia.

Mine.

The tears stop eventually.

Everything stops eventually.

Mouse has climbed into my lap. Walter pulses soft violet like a second heartbeat.

Six men still touching me. Still here.

I look at the wall.

Our story in light. Beginning to now.

Not an ending. Just a place to breathe.

I close the journal. Tuck it against my chest where it's going to live from now on.

"Let's go," I say.

Kieran's hand finds mine. "Wherever you want."

I look once more at the wall. At the image of us — broken and rebuilt and somehow still standing.

Then I turn toward the door.

Mouse at my side, Walter above.

My men fall into step around me.

And I know that I'll never be alone again.

THE END...

BONUS CHAPTER

Let's be honest: you earned this.
And you didn't really think I'd make you go home without the beach scene,
did you?
Didn't think so.

BONUS: KAIA

Three Years Later

The southern coast is even more beautiful than Kieran described.

White sand that squeaks under my feet. Water so clear I can see straight to the bottom. The kind of warmth that sinks into your bones and stays, just like he promised all those years ago.

We've been coming here every year since the Gate. Same week. Same stretch of beach. Same house that started as Aspen's "shade structure" and somehow became a villa with seven bedrooms we never use because we all end up in the same one anyway.

Three years.

Three years of healing. Of learning how to exist without something hunting us. Of figuring out what we are when we're not fighting for our lives.

Turns out we're this: a family. A weird, tangled, intensely sexual family who loves each other in ways that would make most people's heads explode.

I regret nothing.

Mouse is sprawled across the porch railing, tail flicking in the afternoon heat. Walter bobs lazily near the roofline, pulsing soft violet. The two of them have opinions about our annual tradition, but they keep those opinions to themselves.

Mostly.

I've just come up from the water. Salt drying on my skin, sun warm on my shoulders, the kind of relaxed that used to feel impossible. My swimsuit is still damp, clinging in ways that would've embarrassed me once.

Now I just think about how quickly it's coming off.

The house is quiet when I push through the front door.

Too quiet.

I know that quiet.

I find them in the living room.

Finn and Malrik.

Already tangled up in each other on the massive couch Aspen built specifically for... group activities.

Finn's straddling Malrik's lap, shirt gone, head thrown back as Malrik's mouth works down his throat. Malrik's hands are buried in Finn's wild auburn hair, controlling the angle, controlling everything. The way he always does.

They don't stop when I walk in.

Malrik's silver eyes flick to me over Finn's shoulder. His mouth curves against Finn's skin. Slow. Knowing.

"Took you long enough," he murmurs.

Finn twists to look at me. His green eyes are glazed, cheeks flushed, lips swollen and bitten red. Three years together and he still looks at me like I'm the best thing he's ever seen.

"Hey, Trouble." His voice is wrecked already. "Enjoy the show?"

I don't move. Not yet.

I lean against the doorframe and watch.

Because this — watching them — never gets old. The way Finn melts under Malrik's hands like he was made for it. The way Malrik's control never wavers, even when Finn's grinding down in his lap and making those desperate little sounds. The way they fit together like puzzle pieces, three years of practice turning them into something seamless.

Malrik's hand slides down Finn's spine. Lower. Grips his ass and pulls him closer.

Finn moans. Loud. Shameless.

"More," he breathes. "Mal, please—"

"Patience." Malrik's voice is silk over steel. "We have an audience."

Finn looks at me again. Grins. "She likes watching."

"I know she does." Malrik's eyes meet mine. Dark. Hungry. "Don't you, Nightshade?"

My mouth is dry. "You know I do."

"Then watch."

He pulls Finn's head back by the hair. Exposes his throat. Bites down on the tendon where neck meets shoulder.

Finn's whole body jerks. "*Fuck*—"

"Language."

"Fuck you, language—"

Malrik laughs against his skin. Low and warm and dangerous. His other hand slides around to Finn's front. Presses against the obvious bulge in his pants.

Finn whimpers. Actually whimpers.

Three years ago, that sound would've been desperate. Needy. Terrified of not being enough.

Now it's just want. Pure, confident, secure want.

He knows he's loved. He knows he's chosen. He knows Malrik isn't going anywhere.

So he can fall apart without fear.

I watch Malrik stroke him through the fabric. Watch Finn's hips rock forward, chasing the pressure. Watch them kiss — deep and filthy, all tongue and teeth, the kind of kiss that makes my thighs clench.

"Come here," Malrik says against Finn's mouth. But he's looking at me. "Now."

I go.

They pull me in like I'm the missing piece they've been waiting for.

Finn's mouth finds mine while Malrik's hands work my swimsuit straps down my shoulders. I'm caught between them — Finn's chaos and Malrik's control — and my body responds before my brain catches up. Three years of muscle memory. Three years of knowing exactly how this goes.

"Missed you," Finn breathes against my lips.

"I was gone for an hour."

"Too long." He kisses me deeper. "Way too long."

Malrik peels my swimsuit down to my waist. His mouth finds my shoulder. My neck. The spot behind my ear that makes me shiver.

"She's already wet," he observes. To Finn, not to me. Like I'm not even here. Like I'm just something for them to play with.

I fucking love when he does that.

"She was watching us," Finn says. "Of course she's wet."

"Were you touching yourself in the water, Nightshade?" Malrik's fingers trace down my spine. "Thinking about what we'd do to you when you came inside?"

"Maybe."

"Maybe?" His hand cracks against my ass. Sharp. Sudden. I gasp. "Try again."

"Yes. I was thinking about it."

"What specifically?"

"This." I rock back against him. "Both of you. At once."

Finn groans. "Gods, I love when she says shit like that."

"So do I." Malrik pulls my swimsuit the rest of the way off. I'm naked between them now. Finn still has his pants on. Malrik is fully clothed. The imbalance makes me feel exposed in the best way. "Finn. On your knees."

Finn slides off Malrik's lap and drops to the floor without hesitation. He looks up at both of us, green eyes bright, waiting.

"Good boy." Malrik guides me to sit on the edge of the couch, legs spread. "Make her come. I want to watch your mouth on her."

Finn grins. "Yes sir."

He buries his face between my thighs.

Three years ago, Finn ate me out like he was trying to prove something. Desperate. Frantic. Terrified that if he stopped for even a second, I'd realize I didn't want him.

Now he does it like he knows exactly what I need. Confident. Thorough. His tongue finding my clit with practiced precision, two fingers sliding inside and curling just right.

"That's it," Malrik murmurs. He's moved behind me, chest against my back, one hand toying with my nipple while the other grips my chin. Forces me to keep my eyes open. "Watch him. Watch how good he is for you."

I watch.

Finn's eyes are closed. He's lost in it. Making small sounds of pleasure like going down on me is the best thing that's ever happened to him.

His fingers curl. His tongue flicks.

"Mal—" I gasp. "I'm gonna—"

"Not yet." His grip tightens on my chin. "Hold it."

"I can't—"

"You can. You will. Because I'm telling you to."

Finn hums against me. The vibration shoots up my spine.

"Please—"

"Not yet." Malrik's grip tightens on my chin. "You'll come when I say you can come."

"I can't—"

"You can." His mouth brushes my ear. "Look at you. Spread open. Desperate. Finn's mouth on your cunt and you're already begging."

Finn's tongue flicks. I whimper.

"That's it," Malrik murmurs. "Let him taste how wet you are. You're dripping for us, aren't you? Soaking his face."

"Mal—"

"I'm going to fuck you after this. You know that, right? Going to bend you over and slide into all that slick heat and make you take every inch of me." His teeth graze my earlobe. "Going to fuck you so hard you forget your own name. Forget anything exists except my cock inside you."

Finn does something with his fingers. My back arches.

"Finn's so good with his mouth," Malrik continues. Relentless. "Loves eating your pussy. Loves making you fall apart. Look at him — he'd stay down there for hours if I let him."

"Please—" I'm shaking now. Right on the edge. "Malrik, please, I need—"

"I know what you need." His hand slides down. Wraps around my throat. Not squeezing. Just holding. "You need to come. You need Finn to make you come while I watch. And then you need me to fuck you until you can't walk straight."

"Yes—"

"Then ask nicely."

"Please let me come. Please, Malrik, please—"

"Good girl." He presses a kiss to my temple. Almost sweet. "Now. Come now."

I shatter.

And as the orgasm rips through me, I do something I've learned over three years of practice.

I push it out.

Not just feeling it — *broadcasting* it. Shoving my pleasure through all six bonds like a flare.

Somewhere in the house, someone groans. Someone else swears. A door slams.

Finn's grin spreads against my thigh. "Trouble..."

"What? I didn't do anything," I say, trying to look innocent.

"You absolutely did." He's half-laughing, half-panting, and definitely does *not* believe me. "You just sent that to everyone on purpose."

"They were taking too long."

Malrik's chest rumbles against my back. "Impatient little thing." His mouth finds my ear. "Using your pleasure to call them to you. Making them feel exactly what Finn's mouth does to you."

"Is that a complaint?"

"It's an observation." His hand slides up my throat. Tilts my head back. "Though I do wonder what they're doing right now. Kieran, stroking himself. Torric, probably already walking this direction. Darian..."

"Darian's definitely on his way," Finn says. "I felt him through the bond. He's wrecked."

"Good." I'm still shaking. Still coming down. "That was the point."

Malrik laughs against my skin. Low. Warm. Dangerous. "Our girl's gotten bold."

"I learned from the best."

Finn pulls back, chin slick, grinning like the cat who got the cream. "Told you I've got her."

"You do." Malrik's hand slides into Finn's hair. Gentle. Possessive. "Come here. Let me taste her on you."

Finn rises up on his knees. Malrik leans down.

They kiss over my shoulder. Deep and slow, Malrik licking into Finn's mouth, chasing the taste of me.

I watch them. My two men. My chaos and my control.

"I love you," I breathe. To both of them. To all of us.

Finn smiles against Malrik's mouth. "Love you too, Trouble."

"Always," Malrik adds. Simple. Certain.

The door opens.

Kieran.

He stops in the doorway. Takes in the scene — me naked and flushed, Finn on his knees with his lips swollen, Malrik's hand still in Finn's hair.

His golden eyes go dark.

"Started without me," he says. Not a complaint. An observation.

"You were taking too long." Finn doesn't move from his position. "Snooze, lose."

"I was meditating."

"That's just sleeping with extra steps."

"It is not—"

"Kieran." Malrik's voice cuts through. Calm. Commanding. "Sit down."

Something flickers in Kieran's eyes. A thousand years of power, and he still responds to Malrik's authority. Because he wants to. Because it's easier to let someone else direct when you've spent centuries directing yourself.

He moves to the armchair by the window. Settles into it. Long legs spread. Golden eyes fixed on us.

Watching.

Always watching.

"Don't stop on my account," he says.

"Wasn't planning to." Malrik pulls Finn up onto the couch beside me. "In fact... Kaia. Look at him."

I turn my head. Meet Kieran's gaze.

He's already hard. I can see the outline through his thin linen pants. His hand rests on his thigh, inches away from where he wants to touch.

"Touch yourself," I tell him. "I want to see."

His mouth curves. "Giving orders now?"

"Someone has to. Otherwise you'll just sit there for hours."

"I have excellent self-control."

"I know. It's annoying. Touch yourself, Kieran."

He holds my gaze for a long moment. Testing. Waiting.

Then his hand moves to his cock. Presses down through the fabric. His jaw tightens.

"More," I breathe.

He undoes the laces of his pants. Frees himself.

And gods.

Even after three years, the sight of him makes my mouth water. Long and thick and flushed dark, curving slightly upward like it's already reaching for me. He's big — they all are — but Kieran is *intimidating*. The kind of cock that made me nervous the first time and makes me clench now just looking at it. Heavy. Built like the rest of him — for endurance.

He wraps his hand around himself. Strokes once, slow and deliberate, base to tip, his thumb dragging over the head where he's already leaking.

His eyes never leave mine.

"Like what you see?" Low. Knowing.

"You know I do."

"Then keep watching."

The bond floods with his want. Ancient. Patient. Burning.

"Keep watching him," Malrik murmurs in my ear. "Don't look away. No matter what we do to you."

Finn's hand slides between my thighs. I jerk.

"Eyes on Kieran," Malrik reminds me.

I force myself to keep looking. To watch Kieran stroke himself while Finn's fingers push inside me and Malrik's teeth scrape my neck.

Kieran's rhythm is steady. Controlled. Even now, even with his cock in his hand and his eyes eating me alive, he's in control.

I want to break that control.

"Faster," I tell him.

His strokes speed up. Just slightly.

"Spread your legs more. Let me see."

He does.

"Good." The word comes out breathy. Finn is doing something devastating with his fingers. "You're so pretty like that, Kieran. All spread out. Touching yourself while you watch them touch me."

Something cracks in his expression. A flash of heat beneath all that patience.

"Careful," he warns. Low. Dangerous.

"Or what?"

"Or I'll come over there and show you what a thousand years of patience looks like when it finally runs out."

Finn laughs against my shoulder. "Sounds like a threat."

"It's a promise."

The door opens again.

Torric first. Shirtless already, golden skin gleaming, that perpetual heat rolling off him in waves.

He stops. Looks at me spread out between Finn and Malrik. Looks at Kieran in the chair with his cock in his hand.

"Finally," he growls. "Been waiting for someone to start."

"You could have started without us," Finn points out.

"What's the fun in that?"

Aspen appears behind him. Cool and composed, ice-blue eyes taking in the scene with interest. "We brought wine. Though I'm guessing we should put it on ice for later."

"Much later," Malrik agrees.

And then Darian.

He shoulders past both of them, pulls his shirt over his head in one fluid motion, and drops onto the couch beside me like he owns it.

"Hi," he says. And kisses me.

Not gentle. Not reverent. Not the Darian who used to kneel and wait and apologize for wanting.

This Darian takes. His hand fists in my hair. His tongue sweeps into my mouth. He kisses me like he's been starving for it, even though we fucked this morning against the kitchen counter while Finn cheered us on.

"Missed this," he murmurs against my lips.

"It's been six hours."

"Way too long."

Three years of being loved has turned Darian into a menace. Gone is the guilt, the constant need to earn his place. In its place is confidence. Hunger. A man who knows exactly what he wants and isn't afraid to take it.

I love this version of him.

"Kieran's being a voyeur again," Darian says without looking. "Someone should do something about that."

"I'm not being a voyeur. I'm participating from a distance."

"That's literally what voyeurism is."

"I'm touching myself. That's participation."

"Barely."

Darian pulls back from me. Looks at Kieran. A slow smile spreads across his face.

Oh no.

Oh *yes*.

"Kieran." Darian's voice drops. Intimate. Dangerous. "Come here."

The room goes still.

This is new.

Not entirely — there have been moments over the past three years. Charged glances. Accidental touches that lasted too long. The tension between Light and Dragon that started building the night Kieran watched Darian take me apart in that cave. Something shifted then. Something neither of them has ever really acknowledged.

But they've never...

Not directly.

Not like this.

Kieran's hand stills on his cock. His golden eyes fix on Darian. Assessing. Ancient.

"Why?"

"Because I want to touch you." Darian says it simply. Like it's obvious. Like he hasn't just shifted the entire energy of the room. "Because I've wanted to for a while. Because we're all here, and we're all safe, and I'm tired of wondering what you taste like."

Finn makes a strangled sound. "Holy shit."

"Seconded," Torric mutters.

Malrik just watches. Silver eyes gleaming. He knew this was coming. Of course he did. Malrik knows everything.

Kieran doesn't move for a long moment. The bond hums with uncertainty — not fear, just... newness. Even after a thousand years, there are still firsts.

Then he rises from the chair. Tucks himself back in — barely.

He crosses the room.

Darian stands to meet him. They're nearly the same height, but Kieran has centuries of presence that make him feel larger.

"If you're going to do this," Kieran says quietly, "do it properly."

Darian's hand cups the back of Kieran's neck. Pulls him in.

They kiss.

It's slow at first. Exploratory. Two men who have circled each other for years finally colliding.

Kieran's hand comes up to cup Darian's jaw. Darian's fingers tangle in Kieran's dark hair. The kiss deepens. Darian makes a sound — surprised, hungry — and Kieran swallows it.

"Fuck," Finn breathes beside me. "That's... fuck."

I can't speak. I'm too busy watching.

The Light and the Dragon. Darian's golden glow starting to leak from his skin, mixing with Kieran's ancient fire. They're beautiful together. Unexpected. *Right.*

Kieran pulls back first. His breathing is unsteady. For the first time in maybe ever, he looks shaken.

"Well," he manages. "That was..."

"Yeah." Darian grins. Cocky. Delighted. "Want to do it again?"

"Yes."

They crash back together. Harder this time. Kieran's control finally cracking. Darian's confidence meeting it head-on.

Malrik's hand finds the back of my neck. Squeezes.

"Enjoying the show, Nightshade?"

"You have no idea."

"Oh, I have some idea." His other hand slides between my thighs. Finds me soaking. "You're drenched. Just from watching them."

"Can you blame me?"

"Not even slightly." He pushes two fingers inside me. I gasp. "Keep watching. This is just the beginning."

Torric breaks first.

"Alright," he growls. "I've been patient. I'm done."

He crosses the room in three strides, pulls me off the couch, and throws me over his shoulder.

"Torric!"

"Bedroom. Now. All of you."

"Was that an order?" Finn asks, amused.

"Yes."

"Hot."

Torric carries me through the house while the others follow. I catch glimpses upside-down — Kieran and Darian still tangled together, Finn tugging Malrik by the hand, Aspen bringing up the rear with a small smirk.

The bedroom is massive. Has to be. The bed takes up most of the space — a custom creation of Aspen's design, big enough for seven people to sprawl without anyone falling off.

We've tested it thoroughly.

Torric dumps me on the mattress. Crawls over me. His golden eyes are blazing.

"My turn," he says.

"What about—"

"They can watch. Or join. But I'm going first."

He shoves his pants down and I catch a glimpse — thick and blunt and flushed angry red, radiating heat. He's not the longest, but gods, the *girth*. Every time feels like the first time with him.

He doesn't wait for an answer. Just pushes my thighs apart and buries himself inside me in one brutal thrust.

"*Fuck*—" The word tears out of me. The heat of him is unreal. Not just warm — *hot*. Like his fire lives in every part of him, including this. I feel him everywhere, stretching me open, burning in the best way.

"That's it." Torric pulls out. Slams back in. "Take it. Take all of it."

His pace is punishing. No buildup. No teasing. Just raw, desperate need.

Behind us, I hear the others settling. The creak of the bed. The rustle of clothing being removed. Finn's breathless laugh. Malrik's low murmur.

"Torric." Malrik's voice cuts through. "Slow down. Let the others get situated."

"Fuck that."

"Torric."

A growl. But Torric's rhythm slows. Marginally. Enough that I can think again.

"Better." Malrik appears in my field of vision. Naked now. Beautiful. "Kaia. Color?"

"Green." I manage. "So green. Please don't stop."

"We're not stopping." He strokes my hair back from my face. "We're just getting started."

They arrange themselves around me like they've done it a hundred times. Because they have.

Finn settles beside my head, fingers threading through my hair. Aspen takes position on my other side, cool hand stroking my arm. Malrik at the foot of the bed, watching everything with those sharp silver eyes. Kieran and Darian still pressed close together, still exploring this new thing between them.

Torric keeps fucking me. Slower now, but deep. So deep.

"Look at them," Malrik instructs. "Kieran and Darian. Look at what you started."

I turn my head.

They're not kissing anymore. Darian is on his knees between Kieran's thighs, and—

Oh.

Oh *gods*.

Darian has his mouth on Kieran's cock.

Kieran's head is thrown back, one hand fisted in Darian's dark hair, and he's making sounds I've never heard from him. Broken. Overwhelmed. Like a thousand years of control is crumbling under the wet heat of Darian's mouth.

"He's never—" I gasp as Torric hits something inside me that makes stars burst. "Has he ever—"

"Not with a man," Malrik says. "Not in centuries. Darian's the first one he's let close enough."

"Fuck, that's hot."

"I know." Malrik's hand wraps around his own cock. Strokes lazily. "Finn. Go help."

Finn perks up. "Help how?"

"However you want. Surprise me."

This isn't new either — the four of them circling each other. Malrik and Finn are solid, unshakeable, but they've both had their eyes on Kieran and Darian for a while now. We've talked about it late at night, tangled up in each other, whispering fantasies. What it might look like. Who would break first.

Turns out it's all of them. At once.

Finn grins. Presses a kiss to my forehead. "Be right back, Trouble."

He crawls across the bed toward Kieran and Darian. Settles behind Kieran. Starts kissing his neck, his shoulders, his jaw. Kieran shudders.

"Finn—"

"Shh." Finn's voice is warm. Gentle. "Just let us take care of you."

Darian does something with his tongue. Kieran's hips jerk up. Finn holds him down, laughing softly.

"There you go," Finn murmurs. "There's our ancient dragon. All undone for us."

I watch them. Three men tangled together. Finn's mouth on Kieran's skin. Darian's mouth on Kieran's cock. Kieran falling apart between them.

Torric's thrusts get harder. "Eyes on me, sunshine."

I look at him. Golden eyes blazing. Jaw tight with restraint.

"Better." His hand cracks against my thigh. I yelp. "You're mine right now. Understand?"

"Yes—"

"Good girl." He pulls out completely. Flips me onto my stomach. Yanks my hips up. Drives back in.

I scream.

"That's it." His hand tangles in my hair. Pulls my head back. "That's my good girl. You gonna come for me?"

"Yes—"

"Then do it." His other hand snakes around, finds my clit, presses hard. "Come on my cock. Now."

I shatter. The orgasm rips through me, and Torric follows a second later with a roar, flooding me with heat. His hips stutter, grinding deep, wringing out every last pulse.

I'm still shaking when he pulls out. Still trying to remember how to breathe.

Before I can recover, Aspen is there. Rolling me onto my back. Sliding inside with that cool, controlled precision that makes my oversensitive body jolt.

"Shh." His thumb strokes my cheekbone. "Let me bring you back down."

His pace is the opposite of Torric's. Slow. Deliberate. Every stroke hitting exactly where I need it.

Somewhere to my left, I hear Kieran finally break. A ragged sound torn from deep in his chest as he comes down Darian's throat. Finn is still there, still holding him, murmuring praise.

"Good," Finn whispers. "So good, Kieran. You're so fucking hot when you let go."

Malrik appears above me. Strokes my face while Aspen fucks me slow.

"Having fun, Nightshade?"

"Understatement," I manage.

"Good." His hand slides into my hair. Grips. Pulls my head back, exposing my throat. "Because we're nowhere near done."

His mouth finds my neck. Teeth scraping. Biting down on that spot that makes me clench.

The contrast is devastating. Aspen cool and controlled inside me, hitting that perfect angle with every measured stroke. Malrik hot and aggressive above me, marking my throat like he's claiming territory.

"You feel that?" Malrik murmurs against my skin. "How slow he's going? How precise?"

"Yes—"

"He's going to make you come so hard you forget your own name. And I'm going to watch."

Aspen's thumb finds my clit. Circles. Slow. Patient.

"Look at me," Aspen says. Quiet command. "I want to see your face when you fall apart."

I look. Ice-blue eyes. Steady. Certain.

Malrik bites down on my shoulder.

Aspen's thumb presses harder.

I shatter.

Not just a peak — a full-body collapse. The orgasm rolls through me in waves, my back arching off the bed, Aspen's name and Malrik's name tangled together on my lips. I'm shaking, clenching around Aspen, tears leaking from the corners of my eyes.

Aspen follows me over with a soft groan. His composure finally cracking. The sound he makes is quiet, controlled — and somehow the hottest thing I've ever heard.

Malrik gives me exactly thirty seconds to recover.

Then he's flat on his back, pulling me on top of him.

"Ride me," he says. Not a request.

I sink down onto him and we both groan. He's long and perfect and hits everything, and from this angle I control the pace. Control the depth. Control him.

His hands grip my hips, but he lets me set the rhythm.

"There you go," he breathes. "Take what you need."

I ride him slow at first. Savoring. His cock is obscene — pretty in a way that shouldn't be legal. Long and veined and perfectly angled, like it was designed specifically to ruin me.

"You're so wet," he murmurs. "Full of Torric. Full of Aspen. And now full of me."

"Yes—"

"You love this. All of us. Taking turns."

"I love it—"

"Tell me what else you love." His hands tighten on my hips. "Tell me what you want."

From up here, I can see everything. Kieran and Darian tangled together across the bed. Finn watching us with dark eyes, stroking himself slowly. Torric and Aspen recovering, but their gazes fixed on where Malrik and I are joined.

I have all the power right now. On top of him. Surrounded by them.

So I use it.

"I want to watch Finn with you."

Malrik's rhythm stutters. Just for a second.

Most people wouldn't notice. But I've been fucking this man for three years. I know every tell. Every micro-expression. And that tiny stutter? That's Malrik caught off guard. Malrik wanting something he didn't expect me to offer.

"You want that?" His voice is rougher than before.

"I want to watch him take you apart." I roll my hips. Clench around him. "The way you take me apart."

His eyes flash. Something hungry and raw breaking through that perfect control.

"Please," I add. Just to watch him crack further.

He lifts me off him. I whimper at the loss.

"Finn." Malrik's voice carries across the bed, steady despite everything I just saw in his eyes. "Come here."

Finn disentangles himself from Kieran and Darian. Crosses to us. His cock is hard, leaking, desperate for attention.

"What do you need?" he asks.

"Kaia wants to watch." Malrik pulls Finn down beside me on the bed. "So we're going to give her a show."

Watching Malrik fuck Finn is one of my favorite things in any world.

The way Finn goes boneless under him. The way Malrik controls every movement, every sound. The way they fit together like they were made for each other.

Finn is on his back, legs wrapped around Malrik's waist, whimpering with every thrust.

"More—Mal, please—"

"Patience." But Malrik gives him more anyway. Harder. Faster. "Kaia's watching."

Finn turns his head. Meets my eyes. Grins even as he falls apart.

"Enjoying yourself, Trouble?"

"You have no idea."

Darian crawls up beside me. His cock brushes my thigh.

"Mind if I...?"

"God, yes. Please."

He pushes inside me while I watch Finn and Malrik. The dual sensation — Darian filling me, Finn being filled — makes my head spin.

"Look at them," Darian murmurs in my ear. "Look how pretty Finn is when he begs."

"He's beautiful."

"So are you." He thrusts deep. "Watching them while I fuck you. Can you feel it? Through the bond?"

I can. Finn's pleasure bleeding into mine. Malrik's sharp satisfaction. Darian's confident hunger. The whole network of us, tangled together physically and emotionally.

"I'm close," Finn gasps. "Mal, I'm gonna—"

"Wait for Kaia." Malrik's voice is strained. Even he has limits. "She comes first."

Darian's hand finds my clit. "You heard him. Come for us, little shadow."

I do.

The orgasm rips through me, and I feel it cascade through the bond. Finn crying out. Malrik groaning. Darian shuddering behind me.

We all come together. A perfect, devastating wave.

"Okay," Finn pants into the mattress. "That was..."

"Yeah," I agree.

"We should do that more often."

"We literally do it every year."

"More than once a year. Monthly. Weekly. Daily."

"We'd die."

"Worth it."

Kieran laughs. Actually laughs. The sound is rusty but real, and it makes everyone stop and stare.

"What?" he demands.

"Nothing," Darian says. "Just... you laughed. During sex. That's new."

"I'm capable of enjoyment."

"Clearly." Darian gestures at Kieran's softening cock. "Very clearly."

Kieran's expression does something complicated. Then he reaches out and pulls Darian against his chest.

"Thank you," he says quietly. Just for Darian. "For pushing."

"Thank you for letting me."

They kiss again. Softer this time. Sweet.

Torric groans. "Great. Now I'm hard again."

"Already?" Aspen raises an eyebrow.

"Look at them. How are you not hard again?"

"Self-control."

"Liar."

Aspen's mouth twitches. "Perhaps slightly hard."

"Knew it."

Round two.

Kieran finally pulls me into his lap and sinks inside me with a groan that echoes through the bond.

"Three years," he breathes against my forehead. "And you still feel like the first time."

"Good memory?"

"The best." He rolls his hips up. "Though I plan to make many more."

Finn plasters himself against Kieran's back. Starts kissing his neck.

"Room for one more?"

"There's always room for you." Kieran reaches back, tangles his hand in Finn's hair. "Get the oil."

My brain whites out for a second. "Wait—are you going to—"

"Only if you want to watch." Kieran's golden eyes gleam. "Do you want to watch, Kaia? Do you want to see Finn fuck me while I'm inside you?"

I can't speak. I just nod.

Finn's grin is incandescent. "Best anniversary ever."

It's overwhelming.

Kieran inside me. Finn inside Kieran. The three of us moving together in a rhythm that's somehow perfect despite its impossibility.

"Fuck," Finn gasps. "He's so tight. Kaia, you should feel—"

"I can feel it." Through the bond. Through the way Kieran's movements go ragged. Through everything. "Keep going."

Malrik and Torric appear on either side of me. Hands everywhere. Mouths. Malrik's fingers pinching my nipple while Torric's teeth scrape my shoulder.

"Touch her," Malrik instructs Torric. "She's close."

Torric's hand slides between me and Kieran. Finds my clit.

"Come," Malrik orders. "All of you. Together."

We do.

The orgasm crashes through all seven of us. The bond explodes. For one perfect, blinding moment, we're not seven separate people — we're one. Connected. Complete.

Like the Gate, but made of pleasure instead of souls.

Like the alignment, but made of love instead of magic.

Like home.

Bodies are everywhere. The bed was absolutely designed for this, and we're still tangled in ways that can't be comfortable but somehow are.

Kieran has me tucked against his chest, his face buried in my hair. Finn is sprawled across Malrik's lap, half-asleep already. Aspen is doing something complicated with a cooling charm that makes everyone sigh in relief. Torric is starfished across the bottom of the bed, taking up way more space than necessary. Darian is curled against Kieran's other side, their fingers loosely intertwined.

"Same time next year?" Finn mumbles. The same thing he says every year.

"Every year," Kieran responds. The same thing he says back. "For as long as we live."

"That's a lot of years."

"I know." He presses a kiss to my hair. "I'm looking forward to every single one."

The bond hums. Warm. Quiet. Whole.

Mouse appears in the doorway. Stares at all of us with ancient, judgmental eyes.

"Don't look at me like that," I tell him. "You knew what this weekend was."

He flicks his tail. Judgment. Then he picks his way across the bed with careful disdain and curls up on the one pillow nobody's using.

Walter bobs through the wall. Pulses soft violet.

Family. All of us. Even the weird shadow cat and the cosmic jellyfish.

"I love you," I say. To all of them. To no one in particular. To the life we've built from the wreckage of what we survived.

"Love you too, Trouble."

"Always."

"Forever."

"Eternally."

"What they said."

"Same."

Finn snorts. "That's the most romantic shit I've ever heard. Truly. I'm moved."

"Shut up and sleep," Torric grumbles.

"You shut up."

"Both of you shut up," Malrik says.

Silence.

Then, predictably, from Finn: "Make me."

Malrik sighs. The long-suffering sigh of a man who has spent three years managing chaos and wouldn't have it any other way.

I close my eyes.

Three years ago, I saved the world.

Now I get to live in it.

The End.

THANK YOU

I don't really know how to do this.

Goodbyes, I mean. I'm terrible at them. Ask anyone who's ever watched me leave a party—I'll say "I should go" seventeen times and still be there an hour later, somehow deep in conversation about something completely unrelated to why I came in the first place.

But this one matters. So I'm going to try.

Shadows of Change was my debut novel. My first book. The thing I wrote in the margins of my life while convincing myself no one would ever read it.

And then you did.

You read it. You loved it. You told your friends. You left reviews and sent messages and made fan art and asked me when the next book was coming. You fell in love with Kaia and her disasters of men and her chaotic shadow children, and you came back for more.

You made this series bigger than I ever dreamed it could be.

I don't have words for what that means to me. (Which is ironic, since words are literally my job.) But it's true. Every message, every review, every "I stayed up until 3am to finish"—I felt all of it. I still feel it.

Thank you. Truly. From the bottom of my sleep-deprived, coffee-fueled, slightly unhinged writer heart.

Now. About those goodbyes.

I love these characters. I love them in that way writers love the people who live in their heads rent-free for years—fiercely, protectively, and with full awareness of all their worst decisions. I've lived with Kaia and Finn and Malrik and Torric and Aspen and Kieran and Darian for so long that saying goodbye feels like leaving home.

And the shadows...

God, the shadows.

Here's a secret: Bob started as a joke.

I was playing with this idea—what if she had a familiar, but *different*? Not a cat or a raven or whatever fantasy heroines usually get. Something weird. Something that could be creepy but wasn't. Something with personality.

A shadow. A sentient shadow.

And I needed a name. So I asked my daughter what she'd call a friendly shadow.

She said Bob.

Bob.

I laughed for about five minutes. And then I kept it, because of course I did. Of course the ancient Valkyrie warrior soul bound to protect Kaia across centuries would be named *Bob*. Of course the shadow commander with perfect military posture and a judgy salute would answer to the most mundane name imaginable.

It was too perfect not to use.

And then Bob became real. He became the stern, protective, quietly loving presence who held the line for Kaia no matter what. He became the shadow who saluted her goodbye before walking into the light without looking back.

He became one of my favorite characters I've ever written.

All because my daughter said "Bob."

I knew from the beginning how this story ended. I knew Bob and Patricia and Finnick and Linda and Steve and Carl would have to pass through. I knew that was the point—that the whole journey was leading them home.

It was still hard to write.

I cried. Multiple times. Patricia's notebook. Bob's final salute. The way they said goodbye to each other, to the men, to Kaia. I knew it was coming, and it still wrecked me.

But it was the right ending.

They'd been waiting for centuries. Trapped between worlds. Bound to a line they loved but unable to rest. And Kaia—our brave, broken, beautiful Kaia—finally gave them what they needed.

She let them go.

That's what love looks like sometimes. Not holding on. Letting go.

(Mouse and Walter stayed, obviously. Someone has to keep an eye on things. And judge everyone. Mostly judge everyone.)

So yes, this is goodbye. To Arcanum Academy. To Absentia. To the found family that found each other against impossible odds and chose to stay.

But here's the thing about endings: they're not really endings. Not when the story lives in you. Not when you carry the characters with you after you close the book.

Kaia and her men are out there somewhere—on a beach, probably, being disgustingly in love and mildly chaotic. Bob is finally at peace. Patricia's notebook is closed. And somewhere in the cosmic whatever, a bunch of Eds are shuffling around the afterlife, vaguely confused but content.

Thank you for coming on this journey with me.

Thank you for loving them as much as I do.

And thank you for making a debut author's wildest dreams come true.

This isn't goodbye forever. I've got more stories to tell. More chaos to create. More fictional men to ruin your expectations for real ones.

But for now—for Kaia, for the shadows, for all of it—

Thank you.

From the bottom of my heart.

-Zora

ABOUT THE AUTHOR

Zora Stone writes romantasy with teeth: fierce heroines, protective men who'd burn the world for them, and enough emotional wreckage to keep things interesting. When she's not plotting betrayals or steamy chaos, she's drinking iced coffee, dodging laundry, or daydreaming about enchanted forests.

You can find her online at:

Website: ZoraStone.com

TikTok | Instagram: @ZoraStoneAuthor

And on Amazon and Goodreads.

Want behind-the-scenes chaos and sneak peeks? ZoraStone.com/Influencers

ALSO BY ZORA STONE

The Ether Chronicles

Crown of the Mist
Into the Ether
Ashen Oath
Veil of Echoes
Shattering the Void
To the Final End

Arcanum Academy

Shadows of Change
Shadows Rising
Shadows Found
Shadows Revealed

WANT MORE MAGIC, MORE CHAOS, AND ANOTHER DISASTER GIRL WITH TOO MANY MEN?

Step into my next series — **The Ether Chronicles** — beginning with *Crown of the Mist.*
Here's Chapter One.
(Now's a great time to fall in love with a new set of emotionally damaged men.)

BREE

I trudge down the cracked sidewalk, my feet aching in my worn-out sneakers. The late afternoon sun casts long shadows that make the rundown buildings loom like disapproving giants. Every breath brings a mix of exhaust fumes, rotting garbage, and the sickly-sweet scent of the flowering weeds pushing through the concrete.

Just another glamorous day in paradise.

My skin prickles before I hear them. The car engine slows, and then—

"Hey, sweetheart! Why don't you smile for me?"

I keep my eyes fixed on the ground, counting cracks in the sidewalk. *One, two, three.* My hands curl into fists inside my pockets, nails biting into my palms. *Four, five, six.*

"C'mon, baby, don't be like that!"

Their laughter follows me around the corner, sticky and unwanted like everything else today. I resist the urge to look over my shoulder, to check if they're following.

Almost home. Just a few more blocks.

As I walk, my mind drifts back to my shift at Maple Grove. Mrs. Henderson's arthritis was acting up again, her gnarled fingers trembling as she tried to hold her fork. I'd helped her eat, pretending not to notice the tears of frustration in her eyes. Then Mr. Jacobs had another episode. I'd spent half the morning coaxing him back to reality, reminding him where he was, who I was. "You look just like my Sarah," he'd said, patting my hand. "She always took such good care of me." The weariness settles deep in my bones, a familiar ache that never quite goes away.

I fish my keys out of my bag as I approach my building. The Ridgeview Apartments—or as I like to call it, The Shoe Box. It's not much, but it's mine. Sort of. As long as I can keep scraping together rent each month.

I'm still digging for my keys when I feel it—that prickle on the back of my neck that makes my stomach clench. I glance up, and there he is. Phil, my illustrious landlord, leaning against his doorway about twenty feet away. His bloodshot eyes creep over me like insects, making my skin crawl. The sharp, sour stench of alcohol reaches me before his words do. An open beer bottle dangles from his meaty fingers—probably not his first, definitely not his last. His shirt is rumpled and stained, stretched tight across his gut like plastic wrap over spoiled meat. A leer spreads across his face as our eyes meet, and I have to suppress a shudder.

Great. Just what I need to cap off this stellar day.

"Evening, Bree," he slurs, lifting his bottle in a mock salute. "Looking good, as always."

I grit my teeth, willing my hands not to shake as I finally close my fingers around my keys. "Hi, Phil," I mutter, not bothering to hide the ice in my voice.

He pushes off from the doorframe, swaying slightly as he takes a step toward me. "How about you and me have a little chat about this month's rent?" His grin widens, revealing yellowed teeth. "I'm sure we could work something out."

My stomach turns. I know exactly what kind of "arrangement" he's hinting at. The same one he's been pushing since I moved in.

"I'll have it by Friday," I say, fumbling with my keys. "Just like we agreed."

Phil chuckles, a low, unpleasant sound. "Come on now, don't be like that. I'm trying to help you out here." He takes another step closer, and I can see the sheen of sweat on his forehead. "Pretty girl like you shouldn't have to worry about money."

I back away, my heart pounding. "I said I'll have it Friday."

The lock sticks, as usual. I jiggle the key, muttering under my breath until it finally gives. "Night," I yell at Phil without looking back as the door creaks open, and I step into the musty silence of my studio. Home sweet home.

I kick off my shoes and collapse onto the sagging couch, staring up at the water-stained ceiling. Another night alone stretches out before me. No texts, no calls. The guys are probably hanging out at home, laughing, sharing beers. Maybe one of them found a nice girl. A familiar ache blooms in my chest, but I push it away. It's better this way. They don't need me holding them back. That's really all I've done for them over the last eighteen years. And really, they're better off without me. They all deserve to find someone to love, who makes them happy and makes them better. I know that kind of thing exists. Probably.

Just not for me.

I roll onto my side, curling into myself. The silence presses in, broken only by the hum of the ancient refrigerator and the muffled sounds of my neighbors arguing through the paper-thin walls. This is fine. This is what

I wanted, right? No complications, no one to disappoint. No one to hurt me again.

I close my eyes, trying to ignore the whisper in the back of my mind. The one that sounds suspiciously like longing. Like regret.

A faint shimmer catches my attention, and I open my eyes to see tendrils of mist curling at the edges of my vision. My breath catches. Not now. Please, not now. I'm too tired for this.

The mist lingers at the edges of the room, silent and watching, like a presence waiting to be acknowledged. It's always there in moments like this, when I'm alone with my thoughts. Watching. Waiting. For what, I've never known.

"Just go away," I whisper.

It lingers for a moment longer, then dissipates into nothing, leaving me alone with the silence and my thoughts.

I bury my face in my hands, willing the events of the day, the guys, to calm in my mind. I'm failing spectacularly when a knock at the door makes me jump.

"Bree?" Rhett's voice cuts through the haze like a lifeline I'm not sure I deserve. "You in there?"

I squeeze my eyes shut, debating whether to answer. Silence is safer. Silence means no one gets too close. Maybe if I wait long enough, he'll leave—like everyone else always does.

"Bree." Lower this time, but with that edge of steel that makes my stomach flip. "I know you're there. Open up."

When I pull open the door, he fills the frame like he always has, steady and solid and so frustratingly present. His sharp green eyes scan my face, and something in his expression softens just enough to make my chest ache. I step out quickly, pulling the door shut behind me before he can peek inside. He's never been in my apartment, none of them have. Some walls need to stay up.

His presence fills the narrow hallway, and I press myself against the doorframe, trying to maintain distance even as part of me aches to lean into his warmth. The familiar scent of cedar and smoke wraps around me, making my chest tight with longing.

You okay?" he asks, his voice low.

"Peachy," I mutter, leaning against the doorframe.

He raises an eyebrow. "You look like hell."

"Thanks for the boost of confidence," I snap, though there's no heat behind it.

Rhett exhales and rubs the back of his neck. "Look, I'm not here to argue. I just...wanted to check on you. You didn't answer my texts."

I glance away, guilt twisting in my stomach. "I've been busy."

"Too busy to let me know you're alive?"

"It's not like that."

"Then what is it like?" he asks, his voice soft but insistent. "Because from where I'm standing, it looks a hell of a lot like you're trying to push us all away."

My throat tightens, but I don't have an answer for him. Not one I can say out loud, anyway.

At my silence he just sighs and steps closer, his hand brushing my shoulder. "You don't have to do this alone, Bree," he says quietly. "You never did."

The weight of his words presses down on me, and for a moment, I want to believe him. But I know better.

"I'm fine," I whisper, stepping back into the safety of my apartment. "Really."

Rhett watches me for a long moment, his jaw tightening before he nods. "Sure. Fine."

He turns and walks away, his footsteps echoing down the hall like a countdown I can't stop. Each step drives home how good I am at this—pushing people away, staying safely broken.

I click the door shut and slide down against it, the worn wood rough against my back through my thin shirt. My forehead drops to my knees as I try to breathe through the tightness in my chest. The mist curls around me, its cool tendrils brushing against my skin like a concerned touch I don't deserve. It weaves between my fingers where they grip my legs, persistent and present in a way that makes my throat burn.

"Stop," I whisper, but I'm not sure if I'm talking to the mist or myself. Maybe both. The silence of my apartment presses in, broken only by the steady drip of the leaky faucet and the sound of my ragged breathing.

Something warm slides down my cheek—a tear I didn't give permission to fall. I swipe it away roughly, but more follow, silent betrayals that prove how weak I really am.

Get Crown of the Mist here: https://geni.us/CrownOfTheMist